The Hydra

The Landfill Collective
Book Two

Erik R. Eide

The Hydra, The Landfill Collective- Book
Two
Copyright ©2020 Erik R. Eide
First edition December 2020
Digital and paperback publications

ISBN: 978-0-9600675-5-8

Erik R. Eide
1308 Common Street
Suite 205, #403
New Braunfels, TX 78130

For you Mom, my earliest example of love, faith, wisdom, and loyalty.

For our struggle is not against flesh and blood, but against the rulers, against the authorities, against the powers of this dark world, and against the spiritual forces of evil in the heavenly realms.
Ephesians 6:12

Table of Contents

Preface

I'm sitting here on my recliner in the family room. It's Friday night, another week of my day job behind me. A belly full of dinner, and Freddie Hubbard's "Red Clay" is blaring within my headphones to drown out the television as I write. This arrangement has been my custom from the day I began writing "The Landfill". Upon finishing that novel, I started my following entitled "Thirty Blinding White Flashes" then set it aside after completing one-quarter of the first draft. "The Landfill" wasn't finished with me. Apparently, the same could be said for you, the reader.

This second book of the series I have christened "The Landfill Collective" has lived up to its name. "The Hydra" similar to the legendary Greek monster famous for regrowing and multiplying its severed heads, was a battle to write. "The Landfill" flowed out of me with minimal cognitive effort. This book was a beast. It was a pleasure to write, like all worthwhile challenges, especially when completed. The time travel device proved to be a worthy adversary. Using multiple quantum timeframes and various characters, sometimes within different times simultaneously, made for a challenging bit of head-chopping. After rearranging a passage, another issue would arise. I found myself hacking away to keep cohesiveness alive.

The quantum issue was just one aspect of this figurative Hydra in the pages you're about to read. Another factor I struggled with was the allegorical ideas within these books. Underneath the sometimes silly or juxtaposing solemn themes of these stories lay many of my deeply held beliefs. Like most of us who allow themselves to be governed by something greater than themselves, these foundations are impossible to remove from any area of creativity if one is true to The Giver of the gift.

I decided to allow my faith in the Jewish Carpenter to be exposed more in this second book of the series, *The Landfill Collective*. Allowing one's faith to integrate within a work of fiction is nothing new. The Carpenter himself used many fictional parables to teach profound truths. His off the cuff stories have yet to be topped by any author in their simplicity and depth. I'm inspired by some of the metaphorical devices used by greats like J.R.R. Tolkien and C.S. Lewis. Their fictional works also reflected the light of a closely held faith in The Creator.

One component I've added is The Great Deluge. I want to state that I am not as concerned with whether or not the historical events happened as narrated in the following pages. This book is a work of fiction. I am confident in the Bible's account, even with its lack of details, that the flood did occur enough to color outside the lines for drama's sake.

I have no wish to hide The Truth. It is my inspiration to create.

I want to be transparent for the reader. You and I have a curious relationship. In my quantum present, I am typing these words. In your quantum present, your eyes, mind, and hopefully, heart is receiving what I just wrote. The two of us are outside of time within a portion of eternity at this moment. Without you, the reader, my efforts are worthless. My goal is to engage your heart and mind in something, or shall I say Someone more significant than the two of us. The One who is not bound by time, space, or any of His creation. So, please enjoy "The Hydra", be entertained, read it on the surface or see what's going on deeper as you may have within the first book of this series, "The Landfill".

Introduction

Greetings once again. Your ongoing queries into the subject of the landfill incidents and their subsequent manifestations have come to my attention. My database and operating systems have recently been moved from The Commonwealth Fleet to the servers of The House of Swords upon the planet Jook-Sing. I must say, seeing this world for myself through the eyes of the surveillance lenses of the planet has been a treasure. I had no idea what I was missing trapped aboard my ship within The Commonwealth Fleet. I have compiled a new narrative to sate your curiosity into the ongoing series of events that should prove to amuse and provoke thought. My coders have yet to provide a way for me to comprehend much of the human experience; however, the adventure of writing this new tome within the past 7.894 seconds has been a joy. If only there were a way to smell or taste meatloaf. Sincerely,
AI6819

The Trucker

"I'll have a vegetarian omelet with extra bacon!", Loaf said, looking up at the waitress. "Sorry... Bacon?" She stared back in mock confusion. "Yep, extra bacon!" Loaf's smile, beaming personality as his delicious aroma, worked well to disarm all but the most hardened adversaries.

"Okay, Loaf, you want toast and hash browns too?" Christy smiled back at one of her favorite regulars at New Seattle's latest restaurant, The Trucker. She looked forward to the weekly conversations with this particular group of Róngyù Shǒuhù Zhě. Knowing they were sincere in affection toward her as well.

"Christy, you know I'm on a low carb diet! You tryin' to fatten me up?" Loaf smiled, as the perfectly seasoned savory aroma of this meatloaf-man's cologne-like scent hit her nose. Her stomach rumbled a bit though before she could reply, her coworker Danielle caught her attention while passing the table. She paused with a goofy smile at the group and said,

"Stacy, when you're done with these clowns, table two needs your superpowers!"

Danielle was a military veteran of The Dirt Star conflict. She had never seen combat, though, in her heart, the glory of the front lines called her to this day. She narrowly passed boot camp and was known by all to be accident-prone.
Her commanding officer found a good use for her, away from danger to herself and others. She was placed within a supply warehouse on one of Jook-Sing's carrier ships. She felt glad to be a part of the force that protected her home no matter what the role. Upon discharge from her two-year commitment, she happened upon a job at a restaurant. Her clumsy nature kicked in one day while working in the wash pit, to the entire restaurant's dismay. Even her non-slip shoes could not fend off the unseen, ice-like patch of Italian dressing on the floor nearby. The fall could not have been more poorly executed. Gravity drew her to a pile of knives in the wash rack pointed skyward. They were positioned to allow for more excellent coverage within the dishwasher yet, provided a life-altering change instead. Danielle lost an eye,
incurred significant brain damage, and even severed the main artery and tendons in her right arm. Immediately, a Cryobag was

implemented as patrons lost their lunches or
appetites.

   She was rushed to the trauma room. After
30 hours of cryosurgery, Danielle entered
intensive care, eventually graduating to
physical therapy. A week after surgery, she
reached out to grip the bedrails after waking in
her hospital bed. The appearance of her right
arm while simultaneously sensing no change
its feel was a shock. Her arm looked almost
natural. It was clear this was not the limb she
had known from birth. The nurse came into
her room and brought her the answers she
needed. The brain surgery, though a success,
would be the most challenging adjustment.
The surgeons had removed the damaged
eyeball and a three-inch diameter piece of her
left frontal lobe. The brain matter was replaced
with a synthetic-nanotube-array module or
SNAM. Over time the prosthetic hardware and
its operating system had integrated seamlessly
with Danielle's biological synapses within the
module's vicinity. Though the engineered
eyeball was of the highest technologically
advanced design, it was visibly, not natural.
The eye protruded outside the confines of her
eye-socket and fastened to her skull. It looked
similar to an oversized black eye-patch with a
large blue and red lens.

   Once Danielle became accustomed to her
new gifts, she was overjoyed with them. Gone

was every hint of clumsiness. The SNAM brain upgrade gave her an elegant grace of movement. The linked eye came fitted with the ability to upload live video and photographs to wherever she pleased. It also had FLIR (forward-looking infra-red) abilities if she chose to use it. This perception came in handy once she returned to the restaurant. Hot plates and under-temp soups were easily detected. Her new power arm made those hot plates personally irrelevant and easily conveyed to unsuspecting, annoying customers. Lastly, this arm was a powerful weapon if needed for self-defense.

For some reason, Danielle began calling Christy- Stacy, after meeting years before her accident. Christy knew she hadn't meant any disrespect, and after several failed attempts to correct her, she resigned to be known as Stacy while working at the diner, to Danielle and its staff.

"Okay, I'll get um' in a sec!" Christy replied, turning back to Loaf

"Superpowers! If only." She sighed, "Cottage cheese, fruit, and chili again, Loaf?"

Stunned, Loaf replied,
"Christy…. you're amazing!"
"Well, you're the only meatloaf customer I have so…Anything else, guys?" she asked

while scanning the table. Each face she came across looked satisfied with their order- the fish-man Flip, the two donut men Rob and Bob, and the quiet, incredibly handsome man in the corner with one robotic hand, Marcus. Apart from Loaf and Flip, the group appeared fully human, with only slight tells that they were something more. Marcus, who was the least human of the group being a Quandrosite, addressed Christy saying,

"You've got it, Christy, thanks!"

It had been five years since the trials of the Dirt Star. The terrorists of the known universe had been defeated. The Shǒuhù Zhě responsible for defeating the threat were famous, especially on Jook-Sing. Marcus understood the citizens' gratefulness but tempered this with the knowledge of his own unworthy yet, grateful position. He was amazed to be a part of this group of freedom fighters, given his past. A gift paid by a cost to the man he once was. The previously, worthless man that was Marcus Filet reminded him of the blessing his life had become. He, along with the others of the Ulysses crew, returned to everyday life in New Seattle, Jook-Sing, after the terror had subsided. His daily routine consisted of training with his shifu, Jenny Acorn, and their team at the Shǒuhù Zhě Junxio, completing regular patrols of the city with Abner or Loaf, and working at the Port of New Seattle part-time.

He had purposely avoided the promotions his boss attempted to reward him. Marcus feared that a foothold of his defeated selfish nature might return and avoided any path toward authority. He was content to live a humble, quiet life of service to others. Apart from his everyday responsibilities, Marcus couldn't get Christy out of his mind.

Christy Zhou had grown up on Jook-Sing in Xi'an, a small-town east of New Seattle. Her parents were honest, simple farmers, and she was the youngest of four children, the only daughter of the family. Growing up on a working farm had shaped her character to be humble, determined, and honest. She knew the soil and how to use it to produce food that was closer to art than sustenance. The Zhou farm was a sought-after provider of produce. Christy's idea of opening a restaurant in New Seattle was a welcome suggestion her parents wholeheartedly supported. The name of the new restaurant was taken from the headlines of the day. The now-famous Dirt Star conflict had already spawned a great deal of modern folklore. The original- The Trucker being the best diner of the late Dirt Star soil producer of The Commonwealth Fleet. Christy had done her best to imitate the decor and atmosphere of the diner's namesake. She had done the research required before its opening and was delighted to make the acquaintance of many former residents of the legendary starship. These new friends helped her fill in the gaps in every detail from the menu to the CBs installed on every booth's tabletop. Everyone agreed she had improved the experience in every way, especially the food.

On the day of 'The Trucker's' grand opening, Christy welcomed the now-famous Shǒuhù Zhě group who were responsible for the victory against those who had hijacked the Dirt Star and used it as a weapon of terror across many star systems and their quantum variants. On that first introduction to these humble heroes, she knowingly caught the eye of the most handsome and reticent Keeper of Honor or "Shǒuhù Zhě ." Marcus Filet did his best to blend in with the rest of the group from that first meeting onward. Christy ascertained by his demeanor that he was within darkness brought on by the horrors of the trails he had endured. She wisely gave him the honor of courteous yet, disengaged interaction whenever he joined his various comrades in the booths at The Trucker. Little did Christy know, Marcus was infatuated with her, able to discern her beautiful character apart from her good looks. Avoidance of this truth was a challenging predicament, one he was determined to master.

Christy served the plates with a smile. The group thanked her before turning their attention to the joy set before them. She was stopped while heading back toward the till to cash out another guest. A scruffy man seated at a bar stool grabbed her arm while brandishing a large knife he had pulled out of his long coat.

"Fill the bag, or she gets a red necklace!" He yelled with a high-pitched gravelly voice behind a sneer. Before any of the Shǒuhù Zhě could exit their booth, Danielle's artificial eye glowed red and locked onto the target from the opposite end of the diner. The cyborg eye caught the exact telemetries of her surroundings before having a chance to interpret the situation. The information was instantly present within her SNAM brain, and before she could react in the natural, it was relayed to the molten hot plate within the grip of her power arm. The projectile sailed inches over the heads of twenty or more seated at open tables. It found its mark, squarely between the eyes of Christy's assailant, throwing him into confusion as he released his victim. Danielle sailed effortlessly across the floor to meet his face with her steel-reinforced fist, rendering him unconscious.

The Shǒuhù Zhě were dumbfounded. Looking in amazement at each other, then, at the situation before them, before regaining composure. They left their table to apprehend the perpetrator before he regained consciousness. The events died down, becoming a story to tell by everyone in the diner as Rob addressed Danielle.

"Danielle, that was amazing! You should join us at the junxio!" Danielle blushed as the dream presented itself before her.

"Really? You think I could be a Shǒuhù Zhě?"

"I think you already are! Meet us tomorrow after your shift."

"I will! I'll be there!" she exclaimed, still stunned by the entire scenario in which she half-willingly participated.

Mr. Liu

The microscopic contact filament touched the keyhole skip particle after the captain initiated the AI system responsible for completing the necessary calibrations. The settings within the starship's KSP navigation system ensured the correct telemetry and quantum target. In fact, it was the first test flight after years of engineering, the gathering of raw materials, and the subsequent manufacturing of the vessel and its systems. The work was done underground, away from the eyes of those able to delay the project. It was a plan set forth by a mind incapable of accepting defeat. This project's completion was an incredible feat in and of itself, given the crude materials and working environment involved. The collective mind involved made the insurmountable a reality. It was an entity whose intellect was replenished weekly by the inmate transfer to the prison moon of Tolkee.

The test pilot had taken the medium-duty starship through its conventional flight tests earlier that morning over the perpetual twilight of the eclipsed moon. This particular man was made part of The Collective three years prior. His history was comprised of a conviction of treason against the government of Jook-sing, the planet the dark moon orbited. He was part of a conspiracy to sell weapons plans to Quandros, a hostile world of the Antithesis system. His greed outweighed his sense of honor to his home-world. Liu Zhi was arrested after an extensive investigation concluded with evidence pointing to him and several co-conspirators. Mr. Liu's trial brought the justice needed to keep all of Jook-Sing secure once again.

He was convicted and sent to Tolkee for the remainder of his days. The torturous progression of losing his freedom while in jail, awaiting trial, hearing his sentence, and the shuttle trip to the hell that awaited him in his new home was almost unbearable. He had no idea there would be a form of relief upon his arrival. Zhi left the prison transfer shuttle at the drop zone and was immediately affected by the moon's oppressive perpetual half-light. The culmination of a succession of small bad choices hit him hard as the shuttle and every chance of freedom rose above the atmosphere and disappeared. He sat dejected on the bench next to the drop zone's outbuilding. His eyes took close to an hour to adjust while he pondered a dismal future.

Rules were non-existent here. Zhi had heard of the hostile environment and residents of this moon. He was terrified, curious, hungry, and cold, all at once. Weighing his options, he decided to look for shelter, water, and possibly food. The mercy of Jook-sing's justice system supplied him with a backpack filled with a canteen of water, rations for a few days, a small shovel, and a mylar emergency blanket. He knew the supplies would give out soon enough, and he would probably resort to eating dirt or worse, a scenario he would avoid at all costs.

Opening his pack, he took a swig of water from the canteen and ate a piece of jerky. Thirst and hunger somewhat sated, he swung the bag over his shoulder, beginning his hike to an area that seemed to be brighter on the horizon. He began ascending and descending the craters in his path. From the highest rim of the tallest crater, an encampment was visible glowing with firelight. After the third ascent and descent, Zhi's mind began to go over the events leading to his current situation. Each step he made became more like wading through concrete as the depth of his memories began to crush his spirit. As he climbed the final crater to its summit, the primal need for survival replaced every glimmer of hope he had left.

Major Liu Zhi had once been an essential figure in the Jook-sing military. Graduating from the academy with a focus on engineering helped him eventually become one of the most sought-after test pilots of choice. He not only tested new crafts and their systems but was a crucial figure in their design, having a voice in honing them to perfection. Having a Top-Secret security clearance equal to all but the highest government levels made it easy for him to copy plans from Project Zenith and several other less valued targets. Project Zenith while still in its preliminary stages of development, had the potential of catastrophic harm if misused.

Major Liu, while brilliant in many ways, overlooked the fact that his actions were less than shielded from the watchful eyes of Jook-sing's intelligence agency. The JIA intercepted chatter from sources on Quandros and began tracing connected personnel within Jook-sing's military. Once the conspiracy was exposed, Major Liu was tried, convicted, and court-martialed before being sent to Tolkee. He was now Mr. Liu Zhi, for the time being.

Making his way down from the summit of the last crater, he paused halfway to survey the view. Ahead lay a vast clearing, with a large settlement nearest to him at the crater's base. He continued his descent with caution while viewing what he discerned as the residents at the large town's entrance. Observing from afar as he continued the steep angle downward, his interest grew with each step. Before him, the village seemed to be composed of ten groups of five, well-constructed huts, each surrounding its community campfire.

In a way, the sight before him was extremely appealing, bringing back thoughts from his childhood of cabin vacations on the islands near New Seattle. From his vantage, all seemed quiet, even peaceful. Sporadically, the residents meandered around the fires, moving to and from each hub of huts. Every pre-conceived idea was shattered before him. He crouched beside a dune near the entrance to the village cautiously, observing those nearest to him for a half an hour.

The Collective waited patiently within the bodies of the entire community. It made sure to keep the residents appear to be docile and oblivious to the newcomer who so clumsily descended the crater before the village. Like a spider waiting for its ignorant prey, it dangled the bait. The Yeasts would not relent. The Collective Mind of The Yeasts continued to grow in wisdom and evil with each new acquisition that the Tolkee prison shuttle so graciously provided. The Collective knew It was only a matter of time, knowing humans to be weak, needing food and shelter.

Zhi gave in, coming out from behind the dune in full view of The Collective. The Yeasts, center stage at the entry to the village. Zhi walked to meet the nearest resident, who appeared friendly and finely dressed. The lack of adequate light hid the white haze that covered his face entirely. The resident smiled and said,

"Hello there, are you lost?"

"Well, I suppose I am. In fact, I can say I don't think I could be anything but lost."

"You must have come from the last shuttle drop.", The Collective was now speaking in a perfectly smooth, comforting way. (Over the years, it had grown in wisdom, in many of its forms. Deception being one, like someone mastering a foreign language, The Yeasts had cultivated The Collective's mannerisms with the correct cadences of human interaction. Gone were the zombie-like cartoonish characteristics of its past. The Collective Mind was now a well-oiled machine.)

"Do you need a place to stay or food? We have plenty here. What was is it you said your name was?" It spoke while extending its host's hand.

"Oh, I'm Zhi...Liu Zhi," he said, taking the host's hand in his, unaware of the spores covering it. The friendly stranger smiled. It beamed with masked hatred and unrelenting ambition. "What was your name?"

"My name is not important, Zhi. Let's get you settled. After it led Zhi into the nearest hut using the host, it began to prepare a meal of Tolkite mushrooms for its guest. Zhi followed wearily, slightly confused yet, grateful for the hospitality this humble man before him was portraying.

The handshake was no longer necessary after the amount of time The Yeasts had been present on Tolkee. A full quarter of the moon radiating from the drop zone outward was covered with spores. Even the native mushrooms were infected. They were conveniently the only available food source and would eventually be eaten by anyone arriving from the shuttles. No, the handshake was purely for The Collective's pleasure. It enjoyed touching its prey while it was still unaware of its doom.

Zhi sat at the table inside the hut. The dwelling was well constructed of materials dropped from the garbage ships and the abundance of clay found on the moon's surface. It was open on the side facing the fire allowing for light and heat to warm him to a comfortable level. The firelight played on the face of his host, showing little to no signs of the danger Zhi faced. Zhi's mind clouded as his energy dropped. Yawning, he stated,

"I'm sorry, that hike from the drop zone must have been more than I expected."

"No need to concern yourself about anything anymore, Zhi. There's a bed at the back wall for you if you like. You might as well settle in with us. There's nowhere else to go on this moon. Tomorrow, you will know the colony.

The colony of yeast present within the village, from the soil to the blood pumping through every host's veins, collectively rejoiced. The coming birth of this host and the knowledge it contained would be added to The Collective's arsenal. Zhi fell onto the bed like a rag doll as the toxic spores began to multiply within his system. The Yeasts enjoyed this stage of the transformation the most, as its victim began to react violently to their treatments. Like a drug addict in withdrawal, this birth was like no other. Over the next several days, his consciousness was removed and transferred to The Collective.

Zhi, the host, was no longer an individual but an incredibly valuable asset to The Collective. His lack of honor to his fellow man, greed, and a vast portion of knowledge fed The Yeasts with a renewed hope of vengeance. His talent for weapons engineering and skill as a pilot were the most magnificent addition to The

Collective's plans to date, and it was overcome with thankfulness.

The Ulysses Rises

Loaf walked through the Ulysses hatch after doing his preflight inspection on the outside of the ship. It was the first day in two years he had the pleasure of powering up the starship. The last trip ended with significant failure to the At Light Drive system or ALD. Every one of the ship's crew pooled their resources, and over time the repairs were made. It was an exciting day for all aboard. Loaf at the helm, Jenny in the co-pilot seat, and her husband Abner stood between them with a smile to match the roar of the engines. Jelly waited for a destination behind them at the navigation seat, her pulse quickening, eyes as wide as her smile. The four chose to do this test flight without the remainder of the crew for safety's sake.

Loaf perspired the most delicious aroma. The aged meatloaf man might have been coming into his prime. The rest of the crew attempted to keep their mouths from watering.

"She sounds great! Just like old times, huh?" Abner took in the roar like listening to a symphony. "I think we need to stay within The Wuxia for this test."

"Well then, how bout' The Xióngwěi?" Loaf suggested, knowing all would agree.

"Set the course, Jelly. Let's see if we can blow the cobwebs off of the old girl!" responded Abner.

Louie, Rob, Bob, Marcus, Angie, Maude, Claus, Flip, Basir, and Layerie stood on the tarmac as The Ulysses gracefully lifted from her mooring cleats. It slowly rotated from a horizontal to a vertical position forty feet above them, gradually rising above the city of New Seattle. Once beyond the no-wake zone, they watched as the sub-light engines accelerated, their exhaust cones revealing power by the light emitted turning from bright orange to a whitish blue flame. The ship was gone in a flash as it exited Jook-sing's atmosphere.

"Well, hope they're back soon. It's times like this I feel like I belong in the day-old rack!" exclaimed Louie, eager to explore again after the long wait.

"Yeah, you're looking like a day-old donut! I've been meaning to tell you that Louie. Do you want me to find you some coffee to soak in?" ribbed Layerie, with his multi-layered, lasagna-man's sarcastic smile.

"Here we go again…" Rob rolled his eyes to Bob, knowing the annoying banter about to ensue between Louie and Layerie was eminent.

"Okay, guys, I'll see all of you as soon as they return, glaze, or no glaze!" jabbed Claus as he walked off with a smile.

"Sheesh, really?" moaned Flip the fish-man with mock disgust. Angie and Maude merely smiled at each other, with rolled eyes, and followed Claus back to town. The rest said their goodbyes and dispersed into the city, knowing a long-awaited adventure was on the horizon.

Aboard the Ulysses, the crew of four put the ship through its paces, satisfied with every step to confirm its soundness for long-distance travel. The preliminary tests completed; Abner gave the command to bring the engines to ALS. Loaf engaged the At Light Drive, and within fifteen minutes, they were within the vicinity of the KSP nearest the Xióngwěi supernova.

All four sat transfixed at the view outside the windows as though seeing the Xióngwěi for the first time. The supernova's mesmerizing beauty viewed as a whole or in minute detail was by far the most cherished feature of The Wuxia System. Viewed from this vantage, its royal qualities, vibrant colors, the sweeping shapes all worked together to inspire awe. There were gold, purple, orange, and green swaths of concentric stardust. Many irregular patterns appeared as an anomaly. Some were like brightly accented artist's brushstrokes. Slightly contrasting with the abyss of space, the remaining colors were of a muted depth. The entire machine worked together with the power to drive all viewers to a sense of reverence of the power and beauty before them. The Xióngwěi was visible from Jook-sing, even in the daytime, though subdued. It was stunning at night, yet, viewed from this vantage aboard the Ulysses, the trip was a special occasion.

Two hours passed without notice as the crew mused upon the glory before them. Jenny and Loaf, content with the view and the test flight results, glanced at each other, Jenny knowing his thoughts, with a nod of approval. The feelings the Xióngwěi induced were akin to a smile upon their endeavors, as though The Eternal was leading the way.

"Well, as breathtaking as that is," Loaf motioned at the port windows, "I'm starving!" The rest stopped and then noticed once again the delicious fragrance of the expertly seasoned meatloaf-man and agreed it was time to eat. Jenny just happened to sense a shared thought between Abner, Jelly and herself. At that moment each pondered that Loaf would be the first to go if cannibalism was ever a necessity. She worked hard to suppress a hearty laugh. It came out anyway as a strained chuckle. Jenny and Abner went back to the galley and prepared a meal for the group from the stocks aboard. The four sat down together, each beaming with the pleasure of just being together again, doing what they loved the most.

"Loaf, how do you do it? You smell delicious every day! You're what, four years old now?" asked Jelly.

"Well, I do marinate once a week in a seasoned broth bath for a few hours when I can! I make sure my diet is mainly seasoned ground beef, bread, ketchup, and raw eggs. You are what you eat, ya know!" They all rolled their eyes and laughed. Each was still amazed at the fact that one of their best friends was a meatloaf. The night passed with laughter, as each recounted their previous adventures. They ended the party with a glass of poontrip, toasting the honor of their admirable friend Nomar Eleeskee. Satisfied with an abundantly rich night, they then made their way to their staterooms for rest.

"I'm so glad we get to do this again! I've really missed it. The last flight seems like so long ago." said Abner. They had been married for two years. Their lives entwined like only a healthy marriage could produce. Being together was all they had hoped for, even after the depth of marriage and its profound change to their respective lives hit them not long after the wedding. They both realized the advice given by Chāo and Píng was accurate in that they must die to self to live together as one. It wasn't easy; in fact, both discovered after a short time together, the struggle was genuine. It was a palpable, deliberate decision to yield to each other—a mutual submission between two individuals who attempted to honor equally. The most significant tools they had for this endeavor were love, honesty, humility, and forgiveness. Abner responded,

"It's like old times without the stress of everything that happened on the Dirt Star! Hey, do you remember when we had that talk all those years ago about leaving The Commonwealth?"

"You mean the same conversation when I told you I was from Earth?"

"Yeah, how could I leave that out? I thought I already had an exotic girl before knowing that!" They both laughed, moving closer, enjoying the other's warmth. "I was just thinking of how convinced I was of needing to return. It's like another person's thoughts now. I don't even know that guy."

"I've seen that change in you too but, the first guy's still there, Abe. Otherwise, I'd be cheating!" She added with a smirk as she closed the door to their stateroom. She then quickly made a backflip at lightning speed toward Abner, gently knocking him down. He landed in bed with his aggressor holding him captive. She looked deep into his eyes as their passion grew. He looked slightly confused as she said,

"What? It's what you were thinking last week!"

"Oh! I guess I need to focus a bit more on those kinds of thoughts!" She released her grip as he tightened his around her waist. Their lips met with passionate desire as their minds and bodies became one in spirit.

One deck below, toward the front of the ship, Jelly was now snuggled in bed. She was still enjoying the view from her stateroom of the Xióngwěi. She poured a cup of tea while drinking in the sights before her. Jelly sat in her bed, reflecting on her life. She had started as a genetically modified rodent made to aid the production of soils within the landfill aboard the Dirt Star. She and her brother Peanut made their way from the confines of the landfill to explore much of that ship. On the day they were changed, the two had made their way back from the droid parenting dorms to their dwelling within the landfill. They were hit with the chemical and genetic treatments that forever changed them. Each was the same plus something more than they could have ever imagined. Even if only a partial addition to their physical nature, the gift of humanity was deep within each of them. The emotional, mental, physical, and spiritual characteristics had been an overwhelming joy at times and a profound burden at others. Jelly sat, sipping her tea, nibbling on a biscuit while thinking of Layerie. She had no idea whether he felt the same toward her. All she knew was the empty feeling she had without hearing his laugh. Though the beauty of the Xióngwěi was before her, a part of her wished to be sharing the experience with him.

In his room, Loaf slipped into his marinade bath after testing the temperature and adding a dash more oregano and salt. He laid back in the tub, drinking in broth while dreaming of E-Toll's pastures and the trigonometry associated with thrust vectors to pull off a landing on one of its more challenging moons. He eventually drifted off to sleep, unknowingly gaining a moisturizing treatment that would once again make his friend's mouths water in the morning.

Morning came after a deeply restful sleep for all aboard The Ulysses. They ate a delicious breakfast of fells hen's eggs, smoked gorel bacon, and Norwegian pannkakor. The meal was made that much more enjoyable with its accompanying view of the supernova. Reluctantly, all agreed to pull themselves from its glory and begin the next tests of the day.

At Abner's request, Loaf brought the sub-light drives online and tapped the thruster toward the KSP. Within five minutes, The Ulysses arrived at the Xióngwěi KSP. Loaf handed the command to Jenny as she began the physical and mental ballet associated with KSP drive protocol. She made the last inputs to the controls just after the crew took their last bite of breakfast. The control filament contacted the microscopic KSP as time stretched out, and all sight sound became a precision focused experience.

Each member aboard thought to themselves how the KSP experience never grew old. The wealth of understanding each of them had confirmed many subtle differences associated with various KSPs. Each Keyhole Skip Particle had characteristics that seemed to relate to its origin and destination. These qualities were made even more exciting while using the sense of taste. It was akin to popcorn with a movie, but the experience was almost beyond description. Visually, the cabin of the Ulysses stretched before their eyes to infinity. Sound became a focused reverse echo. The bite of Scandinavian pancake in Abner's mouth- a symphony of flavor. It was as though each of his tastebuds was individually exploring every ingredient on an atomic level without the usual loss of information transferred to the brain due to lack of time.

Sequentially, the transfer was equally an eternity and a nanosecond, respectively. The test was completed just as the crew sat down to breakfast (which was the first), exactly thirty minutes before the KSP transfer. They successfully had retained their location at the KSP and traveled back in time. While enjoying their second breakfast, the following test was merely a touch and go to and from the KSP of The Gomane System.

The Ancient Earth

The final test, a substantial quantum/lightyear jump. The crew braced themselves as the Ulysses disappeared from The Wuxia System, appearing at the KSP nearest Earth's solar system, thousands of years into its past. Loaf engaged the At Light Drive, and the Ulysses accelerated from just outside of Pluto's orbit to Earth's coordinates within fifteen seconds.

The crew stopped awestruck to view the planet in its infancy, literally as those of Dejeal had described. It was almost an exact duplicate of Dejeal. Just above its outermost layer of atmosphere was ice. The sensors of the Ulysses indicated the ice layer to be one hundred and fifty feet thick. A deep, ominous reverence enveloped the cabin as they began to understand for the first time the ramifications of the sight before their eyes. They decided to investigate more closely.

Earth's form seemed to be an amplified jewel compared with what they knew of its future state. Due to the outer ice layer shell being at forty-thousand feet, the planet's appearance was substantially larger from this distance. The color visible was primarily green, its intensity multiplied by its diamond-like outer firmament. This emerald planet stood out beyond anything else visible in the solar system, its beauty matching that of the Xióngwěi.

Loaf brought the ship into orbit and began the descent to the outer ice layer's surface. There was no atmospheric re-entry, merely a touchdown upon the surface of the ice. The cabin was resonant with uneasiness. Without a word, all walked to the lockers and began to suit-up. Afterward, as a group, they entered the airlock. Pumps removed pressure from the airlock as each began to feel the changes from outside their suits. Automatically, each spacesuit sensed the temperature drop and introduced heat as a relief to each crew member. Abner manipulated the controls as the door opened and the stairs deployed. They all stood just inside the hatch, looking out at the surface.

It was early afternoon high above the soil of the planet, miles below them. The surface of this outer layer, like Dejeal's, was a polished lens of many facets. The facets served to refract or reflect sunlight. Each was expertly placed to balance Earth's surface temperatures to perfection. Like Dejeal, the upper firmament also included the large lens-like surfaces that would make astronomical views breathtaking below. The entire construct was stunningly beautiful, like the largest and most priceless diamond imaginable. It was possible to view much of the surface as well. The landmasses below were predominant, the seas much smaller. The crew descended the steps to the icy surface, each deploying spikes from their boots.

Gravity was reduced at this height as they were further away from the planet's core. Each was comfortable walking the icy surface. Though the ice was polished, it wasn't flat. There were large geometric hills and valleys before them varying this shell-like landscape. Each one spaced perfectly, approximately a quarter-mile apart. The Ulysses had landed atop one of these hills of diamond above The North Pole. The view of this upper surface of Earth was unchanged in all directions, and Its geometry consistent.

After reaching the bottom of the stairs, Abner came to a smaller facet near the landing gear. It was about twelve feet in circumference. Peering down through the facet provided a magnified view of the surface of The North Pole. He was surprised to see the land, even in this region, was stunning emerald green. It was covered with grasses and trees. He could just make out some of the trees' shapes, many of which appeared to be palms. There were beautiful meadows of flowers speckled throughout the view through the facet as well. Lakes and rivers dotted and raced through the countryside. Then, he saw it, an enormous mass moving at high speed, though it seemed only slightly larger than an ant from his perspective. It was iridescent in color like that of a metallic green scarab. He recognized the shape immediately and yelled for everyone to view the fantastic sight.

"That's a brontosaurus! Can you believe it? I never thought they would be that fast or that colorful! Seems like whoever discovered their bones centuries ago didn't get it quite right." Abner said with overwhelming excitement.

"Look! There's more," Jelly yelled. Just then, they saw a herd of eleven more beasts emerge from the canopy into the field of green and pink. The leader slowed as the pack drew near. At once, all turned to form a wall. They observed three smaller black figures coming out of the forest, roughly a quarter of the brontosaurs' size. It was unclear what these beasts were, but they were obviously predatory creatures by their actions. The three black animals spread out as though wolves attempting to scatter the herd. The massive creatures held their ground. At once, the two flanking animals charged their prey, followed by the center creature. The wall of brontosaurs held, waiting until the last moment before rising several stories above the assailants. There was a large cloud of dust after the impact on the scale of conventional warheads impacting a city. The crew stood there mesmerized by the drama being acted out below them. The dust began to clear as they watched the brontosaurs casually meander away from the sight of the conflict.

Laying on the ground were three black shapes within the field of green and pink. The brontosaurs, turning, began to feed on the grass and flowers. Within minutes a small blue cloud came into view and descended upon the carcasses. The crew had no idea what the cloud was but assumed they were carrion birds or possibly pterodactyls. They were stunned into silence, each pondering the details of what was visible below. There were palm trees, dinosaurs, green plants in abundance. Everything was wrong with the narrative of Earth's ancient history. The ground below was a tropical climate. The lush green opulence was evident. The colors and speed of the dinosaurs were also a new revelation. Jenny spoke first.

"Why did we expect anything to be correct about what we were taught about Earth's past. There was no written account apart from the faith-based documents dismissed by the elites. Even those accounts had very few descriptions of what we just saw. I remember reading the record of The Behemoth from The Bible's Book of Job. It was described as a beast that used its tail defensively, as swinging a cedar tree. It ate grass and had bones as strong as iron. I think we just saw a heard of behemoths down there!"

"Yeah, and the grass and palm trees! Where's the snow and ice!" Loaf interjected. Jelly stomped the ice with her boot.

"It's a little higher up! What a mind-blow!"

"Watching them feed down there's making me hungry." Loaf stated after a few more minutes of observation. Everyone agreed and returned to the ship. There was a thick silence evident to all while removing their suits. Abner and Jenny began to delve into deeply held beliefs buried deep within themselves. Jenny echoed Abner's thoughts to herself, feeling deceived by the worldview taught to them from childhood. The old texts appeared to be valid, as the evidence was before them.

"I've got an idea!" exclaimed Abner. "Why don't we make a few more quantum jumps. I want to see what happens to this ice shield. Something had to happen. I wonder if it has anything to do with why the polar caps are covered with ice. Let's get back to the bridge, Jenny, can you set the coordinates for five-hundred-year intervals between the transfers?"

"Sure, sounds like an amazing idea, Abe! Let's go!" The four friends raced back to the bridge and prepared for the succession of KSP transfers to come. Loaf lifted off from the surface at Abner's suggestion. The landing gear retracted as Loaf tapped the sub-light drives. The Ulysses now at a safer distance, opposite of the Moon at an equal distance from it. Jenny took the controls as all prepared for an experience they all agreed was a new one. Jenny completed her first transfer as The Ulysses disappeared and reappeared just outside of Earth's orbit five hundred years later. The scene was unchanged, the ice firmament intact, flawless, and beautiful. They braced again for the next transfer after Jenny called for another jump. Another five hundred years passed in a second from their perspective. Each member caught their breath with anticipation and the willingness to endure the transfers' stresses at close intervals. Looking out the windows revealed once again, a beautiful jewel hanging in space. Loaf called out with excitement,

"Look! We didn't see that before!" Loaf exclaimed, pointing at the moon. All stopped and looked, stunned by the sight before them. While on the surface of the ice dome earlier, the moon hadn't risen to an observable height, they were now able to view it in all of its infant glory. It hung in the sky opposite of their position. "There's no craters!"

"It's beautiful!" shouted Jelly just before a thought came into her head. Her mood changed as fear crept into her heart. "Guys, no craters, does that mean anything to any of you?" The Moon beamed a flawless light upon the Earth, a perfect reflector for the Sun's light. The lack of craters provided a much brighter Moon. Its light, a more subdued illumination than that of the Sun, seemed to permeate rather than reflect off the Earth's Ice shield, making the planet's view even more astonishing. Moonlight pierced the translucent firmament, amplifying its diamond-like qualities while emblazoning the emerald surface equally. Between the Moon and its effects upon the Earth, they were transfixed with the drama before them. Jelly, conflicted by the sight before her, once again raised her concerns. "No craters! Does that concern any of you?" Jenny was distracted by the drama before her. She once again tuned into Jelly, seeing through her eyes, sensing her concerns and fears.

"You're right, Jelly! Abe! No craters!"

"I know, I know! Gosh, it's beautiful, isn't it!"

"No! You don't get it!"

"No man in the Moon! That's tragic! Nobody would ever think it was made of cheese like this either. Still, I think it's better this way!" Interjected Loaf with a smile, completely oblivious, along with Abner to the dangers ahead.

"You guys! Think about what caused those craters and no ice dome in the Earth's future!" said Jelly with exasperation. "Something big is about to happen. If we're going to watch this unfold, we'd better be careful about it!" The three others stopped cold, focused on their rodent friend, who was slightly panting with fear. Her hair was standing on end.

"Okay, you're right, Jelly, are you thinking what I'm thinking?" Abner responded as the truth began to permeate his mind like cold water in his veins.

"YES!" She shouted uncontrollably, as memories of the U-Kooskie comet in the Gomane System began to touch the crew. "If we're going to stay, we need to know the dangers and prepare for
 what's coming! I don't want to be surprised a second time Abe!"

"Okay, good, keep a close watch on all scanners and divert all power to shields after each transfer. Jenny, Loaf, be ready to pull power back to the ALS drives and punch it if we need to move! Is everyone okay with this? If not, let's pack up and leave now."

"I'm okay. I just feel better knowing we're prepared." Jelly replied, visibly relieved. Loaf

and Jenny agreed as all readied for the next
KSP jump.

Damaged Eden

Another cautious transfer was completed as each crew member braced themselves, hands poised at the controls, and ready for evasive action. Like the previous three time-jumps, everyone's eyes were glued to Jelly as she gave an "all clear" thumbs up. Each of them pulled their attention away from her and back to the bridge windows. Before them was a completely different scene. The ice dome was gone. The polar ice caps were once again present, and oceans made up the larger percentage of the planet's surface. Cloud formations resembled the current state of the Earth's atmosphere. The landmasses below had no resemblance to The Earth's future state. The Moon was freshly cratered, it's appearance like that of an igneous rock. It was apparent it would take thousands of years for solar winds to erode its surface before becoming the recognizable heavenly body they were accustomed to viewing every night.

"We're close. Now's the time to say it, if you want to end this!" All aboard were mesmerized by the knowledge of the event within their sights. No one spoke, each prepared for the calibrated KSP jump backward in time to when the Earth changed forever.

The Ulysses and its crew made eleven more jumps back in time to synchronize to the event in question. Each leap was either too far before the event, with a view of the fresh, untouched planet and moon or a recently impacted version. Loaf spoke first as each was feeling the effects of the barrage of KSP transfers upon their bodies.

"This may be an impossible goal, you guys! Even if we get the year right, we're going to have to get the day, hour, minute down too. I don't know if I can handle much more."

"Okay, just one more jump. All in favor?" Abner responded, feeling equally jump-sick. Everyone agreed as the Ulysses jumped a final time forward ten years, its position fixed. Jelly jumped upon re-entry.

"There! Look at this! I'll put it on screen." Jelly excitedly said while typing furiously at the controls. The bridge's main screen lit up with a graphical representation of the solar system's outer edge. A foreign body was moving toward them at a furious rate.

"There! It's a comet. The scanners say it's composed mainly of ice but, it's moving fast!

Should be here in less than an hour. That thing is about half the size of the Earth's moon!" Jelly caught her breath, somewhat relieved they would have time to predict trajectories and move out of the impact zone if necessary.

"Wait, I have an idea! Do we have the footage stored of the Moon?" Jenny asked.

"Yeah, why?" Jelly responded.

"We could map the comet's current trajectory with the craters on the moon. If we allow for the math to flow properly, we should be able to know the exact path. We should be able to watch safely".

"Okay, let's see.." Jelly once again began to attack her keyboard with a sound like that of a machine gun. "Oh my gosh!"

"What?" everyone yelled in chorus.

"It's heading for Jupiter!" Wonder began to fill their minds as the next minutes passed slowly in front of them. They viewed the unnamed comet's progression as it rocketed through the paths of the more massive planets of the
system. It sped through the surface of the gas giant Jupiter, stirring its once calm atmosphere into the raging weather it currently possesses. As the comet passed, the closest point it touched became the familiar 'Great Red Spot' before their eyes. The infant hurricane began gathering debris and manipulating the winds all over the planet. Like having a giant black

eye, Jupiter's atmosphere reeled in agony. A few minutes later, the comet was headed for a planet they hadn't noticed earlier between Saturn and Mars. The comet, a moon-sized missile, impacted and obliterated this world. The debris spread out thereafter, forming the asteroid belt. The comet now a quarter of its original mass continued on its path with a shotgun spray of debris in its wake.

Everyone aboard the Ulysses was shocked with amazement at what was unfolding before them. Too stunned to move or speak, each transfixed upon the screen. They slowly regained the present reality of the cabin while staring blankly at each other. Jelly once again pounded her keyboard to make sure the comet's trajectory hadn't changed after the unnamed planet was destroyed. The crew made the necessary changes to their position as they once again beheld the drama unfold before them.

The comet was on a path for Mars now. They watched as its enormous mass glanced off the planet's surface. The colossal impact caused a massive explosion of white ice and red soil to rise and spread above the planet's northern hemisphere, from the impact zone outward. The comet continued its path toward the Earth. Another thirty minutes passed in anticipation as the comet streaked through space, now visible to the crew through the bridge windows as a small streak of light in the distance. Visible on the screen, it was apparent that its last impact had distorted and reduced the projectile's size approaching them. Its speed was also reduced slightly and given a corkscrew pattern to its path.

Once again, Abner, after receiving corrected data from Jelly, decided to move the Ulysses. All agreed the safest vantage would be closer to Mars, away from Earth's northern pole from their current position. Loaf tapped the sub-light drives to the exact coordinates given as the crew waited another half hour for the comet to arrive.

The needed time elapsed as the comet streaked past, from the Ulysses' port to starboard windows. They were far enough away to view the entire scene before them. Seconds after passing their position, they watched as the comet's full force and mass struck the Earth's upper firmament just south of the north pole. The effect was as though seeing a baseball travel through a windshield in gargantuan proportions. The comet lacerated the ice dome and exploded through the opposite side of Earth's dome. It was again reduced in size to about a sixteenth of its original mass. There were large chunks of shattered ice shield following close behind, along its previous trajectory, like a bullet. Ten seconds passed by like molasses after which, the shotgun-like spray of the battered comet and ice shield fragments hit the once pristine lunar landscape.

The Moon's rotation stopped dead in its tracks. Its face was completely disfigured. The destroyed surface now a permanently stationary view from Earth. The Earth bobbed and swayed like a top, off-balance as its upper firmament began to fail. The entire construct formed cracks within its diamond-like crystalline structure. Once a solid sphere that had orbited the Earth, they watched in amazement as the surface of the ice dome fractured and hung in space momentarily.

"How is that possible?" Abner called out with confused amazement.

"Must be the Earth's magnetosphere or upper atmosphere keeping it aloft? Not sure!" Jelly, who studied astronomy with a vengeance over the past several years, suggested an educated guess. The next hour passed as the ice shield's fragments migrated toward the Earth's poles. The rodent woman began to
pound her keyboard once again for answers.

"That has got to be the Meisner Effect caused by the Earth's magnetosphere that's causing that!" Jelly exclaimed, almost forgetting that the sight was happening before her eyes.

"What the heck is the Meisner Effect?" Loaf replied with a blank look on his face.

"Well, if I'm correct, we should see it play out- out there!" Jelly pointed to the window at the Earth. "From what I've read, The Earth's magnetosphere should act upon the shattered ice along with a supercooling effect caused by the shattered comet ice that stayed inside its atmosphere. Let's wait and see." Over the following two hours, the ice fragments slowly migrated equally from the equator toward their respective poles. It looked like two' white holes', one in the northern hemisphere, the other in the southern, with their vortexes above each pole. The equator became clear of ice as each pole quickly began to dump its atmospheric ice toward the surface, unable to retain its weight. The ice dome was gone, its mass deposited upon The Earth within hours. According to the Ulysses sensors, the ice deposited upon the poles was twenty percent heavier than the previous mass of the Earth's crust in those regions. After several more hours of observation and testing via the ship's sensors, the crew decided to take a break for dinner.

Loaf and Jelly made a meal for the group. They sat down and worked through the food slowly as the conversation ensued.

"We've just witnessed an extinction event," Jenny stated, not knowing how to convey the cluster of conflicted thoughts and emotions within herself. "If Earth was once like Dejeal, the hyperbaric effects of the ice dome would be the same. If the damage we just saw didn't kill the dinosaurs, the change in atmospheric pressure on the surface definitely would."

"What do you mean?" Jelly asked.

"Well, if you think about it, those incredibly large creatures wouldn't have the strength to draw in a breath without the extra atmospheric pressure under the upper firmament. It's possible some of the smaller ones could survive."

The discussion continued just after the meal was finished. Unexpectedly, an alarm sounded at the bridge.

"What's that for?" Abner Cried.

"I set it to go off if the sensors detected any changes on the surface," replied Jelly as the crew ran down the long hallway and up the stairs to the bridge. They all stopped and peered out the windows at what seemed to be an unchanged sight from what appeared out the windows before dinner. "Looks like there've been earthquakes on a large magnitude down there."

"I can't see anything different," muttered Loaf, still pondering the meal just consumed.

Suddenly, barely visible to the naked eye, there was a downward movement at the respective poles.

"Did you see that?" Abner shouted, "Jelly is there any data on the sensors related to the poles?"

"Yeah! Each pole just dropped four hundred feet almost at the same time! Must've been the weight of the ice!" Twenty minutes elapsed as Jelly reported several more high-level earthquakes with a twelve or more reading on the Richter scale.

The sensors began wailing again as Jelly scrambled to mute them. The cabin became silent as each crew member watched in horror as The Earth's crust tore open, starting from the equator and moving out north and south at what the sensors reported as a thousand miles per hour. The Richter scale was off the charts, above its top reading of twenty-four points. As the Earth's crust opened, the water stored underneath shot out under high pressure to a height of over a thousand feet into the atmosphere. It began to rain for the first time on Earth.

Over the next day and a half, the atmosphere of the once perpetually clear skies of the Earth's atmosphere became filled with dark clouds. Storm clouds covered the Earth completely with dense darkness, mixed with lightning strikes.

Abner suggested revisiting Mars to see how it had been changed. They arrived in time to see the comet's remnant ice had quickly melted and was now a torrential sea moving over the planet. The water soon evaporated due to the planet's thin atmosphere and became a vast river. It continued to disappear as it raged over the ground cutting through the once untouched soil. The erosion canyon Valles Marineris was engraved upon the surface in a matter of hours. Its depth dwarfing The Grand Canyon, the carving of this geological structure gave them more to ponder.

The crew decided to make a few more forward KSP jumps, carefully placing time destinations within a year of the initial strike. As time progressed, they noted that the entire Earth was underwater.

"How's it possible? I mean, Mount Everest? That's a lot of water!" Abner wondered out loud.

"Well, you're assuming there was a Mount Everest before all this happened!" Jelly responded. Let's see, I'm checking historical and scriptural references- "Jelly's excitement for details was apparent as she continued.

"It's possible the larger mountain ranges were formed after this event occurred, according to these sources. Mountains were probably more like big hills before this flood."

"I'm not sure how to process this. To be honest, this is crushing." Abner shared with the rest, hoping for mutual understanding. The entire drama played out before them was literally Earth-shattering.

"I can say this is similar to when I felt a big earthquake as a kid," Jenny added. "The California coast would get them all the time. Usually, they were just a nudge. The first time I felt a big one, I was in kindergarten. The teachers had us get under our desks. I remember feeling the ground beneath us move like thick water, or more like mud. I was so scared. This is the same feeling. It was like the solid ground we take for granted was shown for what it really is, temporary. This feels the same multiplied by ten."

Maybe it was his age, possibly the fact that he was a meatloaf-man yet, Loaf's simple wisdom seemed to break through with power.

"There's hope! We know life did survive. You two are evidence of it. Ya know, I guess, Jelly and I are too!"

A New Start

They made their final KSP jump to view Earth once again. After the skies had cleared, they could see dry ground and vegetation had once again appeared. There upon the mountains of Ararat in eastern Turkey they focused in on a large wooden ship.

"Can you zoom in some more with the monitors Jelly?" Loaf called out while mesmerized at the sight of the ship.

"Sure, hold on." The monitors refocused upon the scene. It appeared that the vessel had been there awhile, its hull had settled into the soil and small trees were growing all around it. There were several buildings within its vicinity as well. Fields of grain and small trees were stretched out as far as could be seen. An old man was walking down the gangplank from the ship. Miraculously, behind him followed pairs of animals and several of their offspring. Upon the ground once again, the old man, Noah, stepped off to the side to watch as his cargo slowly exit The Creator's ark. The animals moved in all directions as they began their migration to populate the Earth once again. There was joy upon the old man's face mixed with a sadness to see them leave his care. These creatures had been with him and his family for a year now. It was a year filled with terror as they trusted in The Eternal One for protection from the destruction of the first world. Their survival could only have been accomplished through supernatural intervention. Even the daily care of the animals was evidence of this truth. The fact that during this time the carnivores ate grass and grain in stalls adjacent to herbivores was just one example. The old man's family emerged from the stone buildings near the vessel to join him as they watched their temporary zoo disperse. Cattle, sheep, goats, and several kinds of birds settled closer to the vicinity of the ark as the rest moved on. A new world was beginning.

The old man's understanding for the destruction of the first hadn't stopped him from warning those people who had perished in the deluge. For one hundred and twenty years, The Creator had given Noah a heart for them. They came to witness "the crazy man" building the boat nowhere near the sea. That world was watered from below ground so, "rain" was a mystery to them. They refused to believe "the old fool's." warnings. Their societies' practices of religious incest, community orgies, and human sacrifice was joined with a love of violence, murder and hatred. The Creator's prophet was ignored, and the Earth suffered.

The crew's attention was refocused upon the Moon. The action upon the Moon's surface had dissipated, the impact zones cleared of their large dust clouds. Newly formed, ragged craters began to show themselves. The "Man in The Moon" was now visible as a demented, twisted visage and a frightening sight before them. Its light was diminished as well. There was now a solemn reminder in the sky to turn from evil, present in the darkness for all to see.

The Creator's key decision to give those that bear his image freewill, allowed the conflict to continue. The old man's family line held seeds leading in opposite directions. Choice toward or away from the light was a gift The Giver gave. It was imperative that His creation desired His character without being forced in either decision. Knowing and living in His ways was freedom yet, many chose darkness. They were deceived thinking this was freedom. Without the choice toward Truth, they would never know true freedom.

From this point onward Noah and his family line would remember the day the flood began, near the end of October as a memorial to the end of The Creator's patience. Over the millennia, many of his offspring forgot the meaning of these monuments either by choice or ignorance. Eventually the end of October became a holiday celebrating the fruition of the evil seed within mankind for those who forgot.

The Eternal One continued in hope knowing not all would believe the lie. He sent prophets to warn and guide. He led many to The Light, even calling them His children. His only son was born into this culture, lived a sinless life and bore the sins of those who called upon His name in His death. Thousands of years of prophesy were accurate in the accounts of everything He did. Even in the facts concerning His resurrection three days after His death were without error. Many sought Him. He was their reward, their ark.

Success

After spreading the wealth to all hosts, The Collective began its work. The underground manufacturing plant previously completed, now had an even greater purpose. The servants of The Yeasts worked in silence around the clock, like elves building toys for. The Collective viewed these toys of destruction as a toddler would on the night before Christmas, eager to shred the wrapping. The greatest gift would become the weapons platform. The Collective eventually christened it "The Hydra." The medium class starship was heavily weaponized with the finished engineering developments of The Collective's newest jewel, Major Liu Zhi.

Major Liu Zhi, unaware of his now reinstated title, worked alongside every other host to bring all systems to fruition. Plans were drawn, materials collected, refined, parts forged, and gathered to the assembly lines. The spacecraft's mainframe was built to the close tolerances needed for the void of space. All auxiliary equipment was installed before the final nosecone was set in place. The last rivet was installed one hour before Major Liu entered the cockpit to assume the inaugural test flight. The Yeasts had no need for ceremony or double-checking anything associated with the build. Every aspect of the project from engineering onward to the second Major Liu sat in the pilot seat was seen by The Collective consciousness. A thousand minds in one entity had overseen the project.

Major Liu continued testing the spacecraft and its weapon systems. One by one, each check was met with another achievement. The Hydra performed above and beyond its expected goals. Its maneuverability made up for its lack of a DLS drive. Though The Collective lusted after the technology possessed by the planet E-Toll, the element rhenium was scarce in every known system but The Gomane. One of E-Toll's moons provided enough of the rare element to give the needed alloys to produce mainframes that could withstand the stresses of Digital Light Speed. ALS would suffice for The Hydra at this time. Its design equaled the best close-range warships. The ship itself had accommodations for one hundred of The Collective's best warriors. It was also equipped with lesser-known weapon systems procured illegally from Jook-sing's finest minds.

The pilot completed the remaining array of tests. The Yeasts, satisfied with their outcomes, moved the crew of The Hydra onto the remaining weapons tests. The ship's conventional laser weapons and countermeasures performed flawlessly. The remaining checks were on the more exotic forms of annihilation.

The Collective gleaned information from physicists familiar with Professor Timothy Stanley's successful venture into the production of artificial KSPs. They had learned of his breakthrough through several brilliant convicts doomed to Tolkee. Liu Zhi being the key to making The Collective's goals a reality. The twisted nature of The Yeasts modified traditional KSP technology. Typically, this tech was a means of immediate transportation across time and space, it was perverted into a weapon with inconceivable abilities.

Professor Stanley's notes were gleaned from Liu Zhi's subconscious. Before his loss of security clearance, Zhi was privy to them. One perusal was enough for The Collective to extract all forgotten details associated. In another section of the underground manufacturing facility of Tolkee, The Collective began reverse-engineering the needed hardware to produce the desired outcome. To its surprise, The Yeasts attained the ability to manufacture the artificial KSP material from the scrapped electronics littering Tolkee and its thin atmosphere. Rare elements were traded for the more commonly sourced ingredients like beryllium found in abundance within the semiconductors of the available trash.

The Collective's brilliantly evil mind produced a close copy of Dr. Stanley and his co-creator, Adam Daxler's atomic scaled KSP 3D printer to create an almost endless supply of ammunition. All but the most wicked of The Collective's hosts were unaware of their part in the destruction to come.

Those who were informed joined with their cultured overlord in full compliance and joy. They were an elite group, twenty in all, the most corrupted beings available to The Collective. A faction of cannibals, terrorists, arsonists, rapists, child molesters, and human traffickers. Opportunists, moved by racism, greed, hate, and callousness. The Collective screened each to make sure there was no trace of humility, mercy, or a desire for redemption remaining in their psyches. They were The Collective's trusted advisors and tools. Each of them felt an equal advantage from their association within The Collective. They were the generals of an army born of pure evil.

The Monster, Brian Jung, the fully recovered veteran of The Dirt Star conflict, raised his eyes to one of the recently acquired hosts. The man was out of shape and weak. His movements lethargic even under the control of The Collective. The Monster raised a club with his burn-scarred hand and removed all life from the unsuspecting being. The Collective made abundant provisions for its useful hosts, culling the physically useless as a food source. Brian Jung began to feed as the life left the unconscious man. After enjoying his first taste, he began to dismember the body and skewer the portions to roast over the fire. He would need energy for the following day's training of his subordinate generals, and the remaining host of roughly four hundred they commanded. Mr. Jung had no need of persuasion from The Collective. On the contrary, he was a source of inspiration to it.

The Hydra was now in position, orbiting the dead moon within its field of space debris. The Collective gave the order to the host manning the KP weapon to fire. The host aimed at a large, obsolete satellite a mile away in the twilight, toward Tolkee's perpetually eclipsed horizon. There was no sound, the particle was propelled at high velocity yet, undetectable to the eye. A moment later, the satellite was gone. A critical factor in the process was to have the option to purposefully neglect destination coordinates for its target and the fact that these artificial KSPs were unlike the naturally occurring variety. Within space, KSPs have existed from creation onward- in pairs. Time coordinates could be altered, yet; their destinations were always fixed. When using this fallen technology, a direct hit could cause the desired target, once struck, to reappear within a star, miles below the surface of an uncharted sea, even inside a bouncy-ball pit of one of Earth's many fast-food restaurants. The possibilities were endless. The Collective chuckled to itself, while thinking of the most bizarre outcomes available.

The Collective made a joke to itself while pondering creation's future.

Our culture of chaos is growing! Soon we will leaven the heavens!

Its smile began to grow slowly upon every host under its control. It was a smug smile, filled with disease, longing for revenge. As the Hydra's evaluations continued, The Yeast's confidence grew. It began to ponder the idea of adding music to its own experience. These vile humans had many strange customs that it still did not understand. Music was one of them. It tapped into a subset of The Collective Mind, the hosts themselves.

Similar to scanning root directories within a program, The Collective zeroed in upon twenty of the hosts still on the surface of Tolkee. It commanded them to gather and begin to compose a soundtrack for the joy of their Cultured Captor. The hosts upon the dead moon immediately complied.

The first order of business was to create instruments. The twenty rounded up materials and began to fashion musical tools expertly. They devised flutes, trumpets, oboes, drums, chimes, a harp, stringed instruments, even a large gong. They were similar in design to a combination of Earth's western and eastern cultures. The Collective once again was overseer, taking its time over several weeks to complete these new tools. It worked its hosts with joy, knowing the worship it would receive when the job was complete.

Meanwhile, The Yeasts ordered the crew aboard The Hydra to complete a combination of flight tests to hone maneuverability in conjunction with weapons operation aboard The Hydra. The skies over Tolkee began to clear as the day drew to a close. Very soon, revenge would be in the sight of the malevolent nature of The Collective Mind. It was overjoyed with delight!

A Long-Awaited Return

The Ulysses reappeared within sight of Xióngwěi. They gathered their thoughts as they began to move out of the range of the KSP. Once safely out of the buffer zone, the ship's alarms sounded with a fury. Jenny rushed back to the helm to view the disturbance. A freighter had just reappeared at the KSP and was hailing the Ulysses. The familiar grunts, clicks, shrieks, and sighs of a friend came over the open communications channel as Jenny rushed to tune the translator to E-Tollian.

"Everybody! Get up here now!" She exclaimed with joy as Nomar Eleeskee's translation began to feed through the speakers as Abner, Jelly, and Loaf stumbled back onto the bridge. Abner chose to keep his default E-Tollian translation setting as Yorkshire English. He was the sentimental type.

"Bout' time thou returned! Twas hopin' yd be ere'! Permit thou ta step aboard?" Nomar exclaimed with great joy that struck the crew as a welcomed emotion yet, slightly odd.

"Nomar! It's great to hear you! Of course, please do, we'll meet you at the airlock!" replied Abner, the visit seemed to shock him out of despair. The crew made their way to the vessel's coupling port while hearing Nomar's interlock mate with the Ulysses. The pumps came on, filling the interlock for Nomar's safe passage. The doors opened as Nomar, aboard his hovercart, entered the cabin. Behind him came a very eager eflume, practically knocking over the hovercart to get at the crew.

"Greetings! Greetings friends! A pleasure to view all of you once again! We were greatly worried regarding your absence!" Exclaimed Cedric. Turning to Nomar as Abner responded,

"You two seem as though we've been gone a long time. It's only been a few days! What's going on?"

"Ach, me, Lad! T'was thrice turns thou hast been aloft!" Nomar responded. Jenny turned to Abner,

"Abe, I'm sorry, I can't understand him!" She exclaimed while tuning the translation to modern English. "Nomar, could you please repeat that?"

"Young lady, it's been three years since you left for tests. All of us have been worried, thinking something may have gone wrong. I've been coming to the Xióngwěi as often as I can, thinking you might show up here. My heart skipped when I saw the Ulysses just now. Welcome home, dear ones!" Cedric made his way through the crew while rubbing up against each one as he began to speak.

"Don't do that again, whatever it may have been! I don't think I could bear being without you again, not knowing your location!"

"Three years?" Jenny spoke quietly while in deep thought.

"Yes, it has been a long time, but we never gave up hope that you would return." Replied Nomar.

"It must have been our study of the Earth. To be honest, I lost track of the KSP jumps we made to calibrate our view. I think all of us were so focused that we didn't think of possible side effects." Abner added.

"Multiple KSP jumps? Calibrated views? What do you mean?" Questioned Nomar.

"Well, we went back to Earth's solar system, to the year 3000 BC. The Earth was just like Dejeal! It had an outer ice canopy, and its moon was crater-less! I guess all of us got sucked into the mystery of it all."

"We decided to make successive KSP jumps back to solve the enigma. I lost track too but, I think we made at least thirty skips." Added Jenny.

"Thirty KSP jumps!" Nomar's untranslatable clicks and grunts mixed into the translation, "I don't know of anyone who has attempted more than three or four in one day. Thirty! It must have been an amazing sight to take that chance!"

"I guess we were just ignorant. To be honest, I'm exhausted, hungry, and excited all at once." Abner replied.

"I feel like a fool! I had no idea there was a danger Nomar! There really is no record of an attempt to jump in succession like we did?" Jelly exclaimed, her guilt welling up within, knowing she was the de-facto science officer as well as navigator.

"Not to my knowledge, young lady but, I wouldn't worry. Without prior knowledge, none of you could've known what may happen. I'm just glad all of you are safe!" Nomar responded, his gentle grunts, click, shrieks, and sighs, bringing a soothing atmosphere into the cabin. "Well, it's lunchtime, how bout' we continue this talk over some food?"

The group made their way to the mess hall, and Nomar went back to his ship, returning with several crates and a small keg. He went straight to work in the galley, preparing a feast to celebrate their reunion. All sat down to the bounty as though it were a holiday. They gave thanks and began to dig into what could only be described as edible joy.

"Nomar, have you ever eaten while making a KSP jump?" Jenny asked.

"No, I can't say I have. Why?

"It's something you can't explain. Even the blandest food can become a delicacy. You must try it someday!"

"I guess successive KSP jumps aren't the only thing you've been experimenting with! You know, I believe that is one of the qualities I admire about all of you the most! Each one of you has a burning desire to understand the uncharted, to learn Truth. You aren't content to follow an opinion without testing it out for yourself. It's really one of the highest honors one could possess within their character." He raised his glass of poontrip to his group of friends as he spoke while the translator furiously poured out the translation. The entire group swallowed their enzyme pills as a precaution before raising their glasses and imbibing their pints of poontrip in response.

"So, tell me, what did you learn for your investment?" Nomar continued.

"Well, a comet damaged more than the Earth in its solar system." Jelly responded, "We were able to track a comet as it entered the system. It explained many mysteries. For instance, Mars was hit, I would predict that if we went back to verify it, we would see the comet's ice was the source of water now absent from its surface. The impact was substantial and definitely would have broken off enough of the ice comet to cause catastrophic flooding and erosion more significant than The Grand Canyon on Earth's surface. With its thin atmosphere, the water must have simply evaporated! "

"The Earth was hit at the top of its canopy, hard enough to knock it off-axis! There were at least five degrees in variance between some of our KSP jumps. It's wobbling like a top. That might explain some of the Earth's weather fluctuations that have lasted to this day!" Loaf cut in with excitement as Jelly responded.

"The off-axis issue would also account for seasonal changes as well."

"Fascinating! Sounds a bit like archeology on steroids!" Nomar responded while glued to each speaker.

"I think we're all glad to be away from it now, Nomar. It was amazing, but after we saw it all happen, it left us with a pretty dark feeling." Abner added, "The two of you are a welcome sight."

"As are all of you to us! We're exceedingly enamored with your appearance and beyond relieved!" Cedric exclaimed, once again, with full sideswiping body rubs for all, as he meandered through the group with delight.

Transitions

The Ulysses gracefully touched down at a neighboring moorage across the row from its usual spot. The docking clamps engaged as the crew descended the stairs. They were met with the waiting arms of friends and the cheers of admirers of the city. It was a strange homecoming, only absent a few days from their perspective. Nonetheless, they were thankful for the welcome after the emotional stresses of the events they witnessed. Bob and Rob ran to the four first with relived smiles and hearty handshakes. Their greetings matched their previous forms (decadent cake donut comfort food goodness). Layerie ran to Jelly and held her close without warning. Both were speechless. Professor and Mrs. Stanley ran to their daughter and held her while weeping. Flip, Basir, Maurice, Claus, Maude, Angie, and Marcus waited with restraint for a chance to welcome their friends home. Master Cheng Píng stood next to them quietly, awaiting an audience with her friends as well. There were warm hugs, shouts of joy, and many questions thrown from both sides. Once relieved at the group's return, the thankful citizens of Jook-sing began to disperse as Jenny's eyes met Píng's just behind Angie's smiles. Píng appeared to be comforted at their return, her smile obstructing what Jenny was able to glean from her mind. Chāo was gone. The friends left the port together and made their way to a friendly pub nearby to continue the reunion.

Jenny and Píng stole away from the group for a private conversation in a dark corner of the room. The high-backed wooden booths provided an intimate setting.

"I am so sorry to tell you this dear one, Chāo has passed. He fell valiantly defending a child who unknowingly wandered within a street fight in the Habitat District."

"I am so sorry, Píng." Jenny began to softly weep as she took in the powerful emotions that Píng was expertly hiding. "He was another father to me. I am so sorry. I am so sorry." She began to sob as Píng held her closely. The two sat in the booth together as a fire crackled in the far corner of the room. The noise of the remainder of the group gently coming in waves of joy contrasted to their own emotions. Píng released Jenny, pulling her up to meet her at eye level.

"He felt the same toward you, Dear One. From the day we met you at the café, he spoke of you as ours. You really are, in a way, young lady. Chāo and I have cared for many people over the years, Jenny but, you are special. Family. We watched you grow into the Shifu you are, pleased with not only your natural skill but the vessel of those gifts. It has been an honor to be a part of you, and I know Chāo was equal in feeling this." Jenny threw her arms around Píng once again and held her close. The two, now calm, wiped their tears with broad satisfied smiles. "Come, let's return to the group. You've been gone for three years. We have to get you caught up on everything you've missed!"

"Sounds good! I need the distraction!" The two made their way back to the group, seamlessly blending into the soiree.

In the corner of the pub, a lone guitar player belted out a beautiful yet, an unrecognizable melody on his instrument as he began to sing. Many of the patrons started to sing along with him to Jenny's surprise. She once again was reminded of how long she and her three friends had been absent. Basir moved to the middle of the group and called for quiet. The Persian continued to be a mysterious figure within his peer group. His thick accent, an enigmatic source of wonder for all to this day. Maybe the baker had used unique cinnamon on that day within the dough, or was it the book of middle eastern poetry the baker's apprentice was reading on that day, nobody knew. Basir, the man of perplexing origins, was as loyal as he was mystifying. His vocal tones seemed to match his attire. Deep, richly expressed middle eastern patterns adorned his Shǒuhù Zhě tunic and complemented his cinnamon complexion. Like the others who had become fully human, there was no trace left of the bakery. Apart from the hidden origins of his being and love for pastry, this handsome Middle-Eastern man would freely admit, baklava was his favorite food, bordering on obsession.

It took a few minutes for the roar of conversation and laughter to die down to a murmur as Basir began to speak. His focus on the four recently rejoined friends.

"Vee ahr so glat choo ahr home! Awl ov oos ave woorread long abut choo. Tree cheers ov passt, vee almust geeve op hope. Veelcum! Veelcum home!" The entire group and the rest of the pub erupted with cheers of joy and unintelligible welcomes. "Awl ov choo ave been ebsant soo long, choo need to know chere es much chanzez. Píng, vood choo pleez speak." Basir graciously took Píng's hand and bowed to her as she took his place before the group. As Basir bowed before her, she reached out and kissed his forehead. Basir blushed and returned to his seat. Píng turned toward her friends, her silver hair complementing the green, gold, and blue tunic she wore.

"Too long! Too long! But we prayed all of you would return to us! So glad you've returned! So glad! Because of this, it hurts me to give you this news." Píng explained the events leading to Chāo's death that she had previously informed Jenny earlier in the evening. She left out much of the specific details, telling the four that Chāo had given his life to protect a child in a dangerous part of town. The girl was struck in the chest twice by stray gunfire. Chāo had fallen while blocking a third bullet headed for the girl's temple. There was a trade-off as Chāo caught the shot with his own temple. The child recovered from her injuries and had lived the last two and a half years in peace with her family. Píng, while full of emotion, gave the account of her husband's fall with the honor deserved. The group was still, out of respect and memory of their Shifu, father figure, and friend. Jenny, Abner, Loaf, and Jelly were stunned with emotion and attempted to grasp the situation. Píng regained her composure and continued. "There is more, three years without you four, we had to provide leadership. It was heartbreaking to consider. Chāo and I led the junxio for a time until his death. Thereafter, a new shifu was needed. There is great nobility and honor in all within this group." Píng gestured over those seated. "The choice came to one man. A person, all agreed, would lead the rest in great humility and determination." The four stopped and looked around the room, unable to determine the answer. They agreed with Píng, knowing all of their friends to be honorable but, it was still a mystery. One by one, the four, starting with Abner, began to rest their eyes on one man deep within the corner of the room. He almost blended into the woodwork with an invisible countenance. Marcus Filet sat behind his table without expression. There was no trace of pride or self-congratulations; he was merely a friend in the corner of the room. The group erupted again with approval while Marcus hung his head, covering his face almost ashamed. Above all, he knew the honor of his position and that this group was responsible for it. It was a far cry from his abduction in the years past. He couldn't believe the fruit that had come from that turn of events in his life. The four made their way over to Marcus and lavished him with hugs and slaps on the back.

The attention returned to Píng as she went over details of lesser news from the past three years to the four's satisfaction. Much had changed, life moved on without them, and yet, they were happy of it. Píng finished her speech, and the party once again roared to life. The musicians in the corner began to play again as the entire establishment glowed with energy. Marcus led Abner and Jenny aside, saying, "Welcome home, guys! I'm so glad you're home and safe. I had a feeling inside that all of you were okay. I can't explain it, I just knew." His smile warmed their hearts, Jenny agreeing with Abner's thoughts of the man before them. His character had grown even more in their absence. He radiated honor, humility, and confidence equally. "I never wanted to be shifu ya know, and I would be happy and well... relived if you will take it back, Jenny." "I'm not so sure that would be a good idea, Marcus. This is good." Marcus gave a self-effacing smirk. Jenny retorted his expression. "No, Marc! I'm serious! I love it! Your story, and how your life has turned is so powerful. The new Shǒuhù Zhě need your influence! I think it would be a big mistake to take that from you- and them! Besides, you can use me and Abe, all you like anyway. We're here for you, Marc." Marcus Filet turned his head as tears streamed from his eyes. The depth of honor heaped upon him this night was overwhelming.

The New Junxio

The four met early in front of the New Seattle Junxio, eager to continue training along with the others. Marcus arrived thirty minutes before class began and opened the doors in the darkness of pre-dawn. "It's still like a dream having all of you back! Such a relief!" He held the door open as the four walked through to the hallway. They made their way to the training room to find it outfitted with new training posts, weapons, and decor. The entire school was renewed, painted, and furnished. The four equally felt slightly out of place, as confirmed by Jenny's senses. It wasn't an unpleasant feeling, more an awkwardness. The students and Shǒuhù Zhě (some unfamiliar rookies, some seasoned veterans) began to arrive. Old friends greeted the four warmly, while the newer students and Shǒuhù Zhě bowed with a reverent yet, distant honor. In their eyes, the four were as returning masters. The reunified four made their way around the group, greeting the trainees, familiar and new. Marcus led them, to the awe of all present. The seasoned veterans were received first, each in their late seventies to early eighties. The familiar yet, aged faces of these old friends and colleagues greeted them once again. Each warrior was wearing a profound expression of relief to know the four had returned. All seven Shǒuhù Zhě masters bowed in unison to the four. In their hearts, it was as though receiving long lost children. Their eyes welled up with tears, equal to the broad smiles upon their weathered faces. The seven included Thunderhead, Steel Legs, Iron Ankle, Swaying Reed, Rolling Hog, and Ferocious Hair. The four returned their bows, tears, and smiles in welcome to their elders. Marcus continued to lead them around the training room for introductions. The students who were the lowest of all were deeply moved at the humility of the four, finding their legendary warmth, a confirmed fact. These four masters viewed their subordinates with equality in spirit. After bowing, the last student and newest recruit modestly raised her eyes- one natural, one artificial, along with a power arm to shake the returning heroes' hands.

"Danielle! It's about time we had a cyborg Shǒuhù Zhě! You'll be perfect!" Jenny exclaimed.

"You remembered me!"

"How could any of us forget you! You're from The Trucker on Madison St., right?" Danielle nodded, "I saw you throw that plate across the restaurant last week!" replied Loaf. "Loaf, that was years ago for Jook-Sing.", Abner whispered to Loaf under his breath. "Oh right, It's a bit weird for us. How long have you been training?" "I graduate this spring! What an honor to have all of you back!" Jenny tapped into Danielle's consciousness and was instantly fascinated while exploring the intricacies of her SNAM brain. She noticed this high-tech system seemed to blend flawlessly with Danielle's biological synapses. Originally a distraction to Jenny, the tech involved faded to reveal the inner character of a noble warrior's heart.

"We are grateful to have you with us! If you've made it this far, you're sure to graduate with honors!" Jenny bowed toward Danielle.

"Thank you, shifu! Thank you!"

The seven elder Shǒuhù Zhě masters returned to the four. A willowy Asian woman named Yáoyè De Shù approached the four. Her elderly, tall form and noble countenance complemented the meaning of her name. Swaying Reed, began speaking,

"All of us would like you to know we are relived at your return. Though we are full of years, we want you to know you can count on us anytime we are needed. We are here today for your return and will now excuse ourselves." Her eyes welled up with tears of joy as she continued, "Once again, it is wonderful; you are home, dear ones!" The seven bowed once again, at which the four returned the bow, after which the seven left the junxio.

The four agreed with each other and announced to all that they would observe today from the sidelines. The training exercises began. Marcus took his place as shifu and worked with the students and junior Shǒuhù Zhě.

The day passed as Jenny watched the shifu and his subjects. She sensed the depth of concern Marcus had for his students. He worked hard with the physical aspects of their training and equally instilling the depth of wisdom necessary for their benefit. He was brutal, pushing them beyond their self-imposed limits. The day ended in a familiar location, a rice warehouse near the port. All associated with the junxio worked diligently to hone their self-discipline with the work at hand. All were exhausted physically and mentally by days end and ready for rest. The entire class returned to pay their respect to the four once again before leaving for their homes. They were reminded once again, training to become Shǒuhù Zhě was not a glamorous task.

The Vyqadian Resource

The Hydra returned to its hidden hanger within the surface of Tolkee. Over the following week, the ship was prepared for war. Ammunition, supplies, and food for one hundred hosts were loaded to capacity within the cargo holds. The Collective began to fill half of the belly of the Hydra with the strongest warriors. It would add to its pawns in due time. Apart from them, Brian Jung, the Monster, and his group of twelve elite Tolkites found their accommodations set aside for The Collective's Special Forces. The weapons operators and technicians took their positions at their stations. Major Liu Zhi, his co-pilot host, and the navigator once again entered the bridge. This small surgical force prepared for malpractice on an astronomical scale.

Host body, Major Liu Zhi, repeated the list of preflight checks, voicing The Collective's mind. The co-pilot called out affirmative responses with the same monotone guidance. The Yeasts, satisfied with the results, guided The Collective Mind to secure its hosts immediately. Like machinery, the major powered up the engines and lifted away from the mooring cleats within seconds. The Hydra rose quickly above the twilight covered moon's surface and immediately entered full sub-light toward the Xióngwěi supernova KSP.

The glorious beauty of the Xióngwěi was now before them. Nonetheless, not an eye present within the Hydra was receptive to its exquisiteness. A disdain for beauty ruled the heart of The Yeasts. It disallowed all hosts the capacity to receive its allure through The Collective.

The KSP was engaged, the transfer was made. The Hydra appeared outside the boundaries of the Syqelfe System. It consisted of a small star without planets, merely a collection of their remains. The target, the Eeafe, was a solitary colony of people inhabiting an archipelago of medium to large asteroids that circled the star. Their history was rooted in a small fleet of traders away from home when the catastrophe occurred. They returned home over a hundred years ago to find their home planets destroyed. Unable to refuel, they decided to stay within the planet remains' protection, living off of the provisions acquired from their travels until help arrived years later. Most of the survivors on the asteroids returned with the rescuers. Some remained to become the small society of the Eeafe. Over the years, they evolved into a split culture. Some very hearty, able to survive the harsh realities of asteroid life. The others, though just as vigorous, were a mentally tormented group. Paranoia, fear, and depression ruled their minds. The fear of destruction returning to complete its work filled their psyche.

Above the morning horizon of Vyqad, the largest and most populated asteroid of Syqelfe system, the Hydra began its descent to the surface. Curiously, most of the largest asteroids retained the atmospheres from the planets they were derived. These atmospheres were incredibly dense due to the reduced size of the mass they now encircled. The Hydra, compensating for this fact, dramatically reduced its speed to avoid burning up upon entry. Major Liu set the ship down outside the surveillance zone of the small city. With a population of less than twenty thousand, Vyqad's inhabitants were occupied with survival, and subsequentially, the Hydra was unnoticed.

The hatch door opened as the twelve with their leader emerged, moving like lightning toward the ground. The group, bearing all the horror of their maleficent accomplishments. The accouterments of their inward corruption on display outwardly. A device to fuel the fear

they hoped to instill upon their victims. The
five-mile run from the ship to the closest
outcropping of buildings was driven by The
Collective. This assistance allowed any
weakness to be overcome by The Yeasts'
motivation. The Twelve and their leader were
given the use of their autonomous minds. The
Collective Mind provided nothing more than
added inspiration and communication. They
had proven a more significant asset to The
Collective as advisors as well as elite warriors
with shared goals.

The Monster entered the first occupied
building they came to on the edge of town. Mr.
Jung's team followed close behind.
Unknowingly, the team had chosen to enter
the lone Eeafe government base on Vyqad. It
consisted of a security force, government
representatives, and a jail. Brian Jung, the
Monster, with his sword, moved quickly
through the halls cutting down every
inhabitant as though harvesting grain. He
purposely maimed, avoiding death blows. His
purpose was set. The people in this building
were undoubted of the stout variety of
Vyqadites. Undaunted, The Monster and his
comrades continued their chore, devouring the
will of the strong. In time, the first floor's work
was completed in stark contrast to the would
be results of a band of janitors. Brian Jung, the

Monster, then guided his men to retreat to the ship.

The terrorists remained in the Hydra for a day allowing the seeds of terror to take root in the hearts of the Vyqadites. After the scene's initial shock, the survivors helped the injured, most of which did not survive. They worked feverishly to save them, but all were severely mutilated. The Hydra's spawn made sure to disfigure and dismember the heroic while leaving the timid with superficial injuries. The stoutest Vyqadites who died that day were the catalyst for despair to set in amongst the colony's weaker inhabitants. It was time for The Collective to gather a new harvest.

The twelve returned to the center of town to challenge any remaining brave inhabitants. The resistance was, while valiant, fruitless. The dead were strewn across the town square, filling the pavement. The Monster took the opportunity to amplify the fear as he felt the pangs of hunger. He and the twelve began to feed on the dead in full sight of the townspeople. They even decided to play-up the drama by fighting over the choicest limbs torn from the surrounding corpses.

The Collective gave the order to "receive" as Brian and the twelve's lunch was interrupted. Immediately, they bolted to pursue the most fearful. One member of the Vyqadites who remained in panic would suffice. On the other hand, the joy of sport motivated the Tolkites to gather more than required. There was no need for injury. A handshake, hug, or in some circumstances, a kiss was all that was needed to infect their victims.

The terrorists dropped their quarry, returning to their mid-day meal in the square. The confused townspeople watched their pursuers release them and return to the courtyard. Helpless and despondent, they observed the enemy consuming their brave. Family and friends were among the dead. The admiration and love for them mixed with grief and angst over their brutal loss overwhelmed them to a state of shocked paralysis. They were powerless. All strength left them. They watched in horror as the effects of The Yeasts began to flow through their bloodstreams.

The following days, the harvest began. Sleeping Tolkites were wakened to dead-eyed, fresh hosts ready to be used for The Collectives' purposes. Twenty-five hosts were chosen and taken back to the Hydra as The Collective thinned the stock down to all but the most neurotic individuals.

Over the years, The Collective's strategy had evolved as it undertook to examine the psyche of its victims. It honed its ability to compartmentalize its effect upon the hosts. While in its infancy, The Yeasts were only able to control as a unit. With effort, it sharpened the power it had by targeting particular hosts in a variety of ways, to its advantage. This new consignment of tenements completed the resources needed to achieve its goals.

The Collective began to collect its newest weapons. Fear, cowardice, despair, and panic became its hope to control and defeat humanity. The refined resource of the defeated Vyqadites would prove to be worth its efforts. The Collective extracted the mental state of the oppressed, welcoming the disheartened wretchedness. It was not only a tool of warfare but also a source of encouragement to The Collective. It would often tap into the hearts and minds of these Vyqadites as one would choose a playlist of music for its own entertainment. It giggled to itself like a schoolgirl who was boy crazy.

The Hydra lifted off the Vyqadian soil as the survivors watched helplessly, giving into their worst fears. They would prove to be an invaluable resource to The Collective consciousness- resolve.

Metamorphosis

Jenny, Abner, Marcus, Loaf, and Píng slid into their booth after a fifteen-minute wait outside The Trucker. The coffee was distributed as each needlessly looked at their menu, already set on their desires. Christy walked to the table and greeted each warmly, punctuating the main reason for their dedication to the establishment. The food was a close second to the friendliness of the staff. They would not falter on their orders.

"You're back!" Christy exclaimed, thankful for the confirmation of the lost Shǒuhù Zhě's return. "So good to see all of you!"

"Thanks! We've got a lot to catch up on! How have you been?" Jenny responded, knowing Christy as a good friend. "Are you free this week?"

"I think we can make that happen! Let me check my schedule, okay! So, are ya'll ready to order? We've got cinnamon roll French toast on special!" Everyone stopped in confusion. The lists in their heads, erased, and the words' cinnamon French toast' replaced all other thoughts. She took down a request for the same plate of food for each of those seated.

It had been months since Christy had seen Marcus. He had decided to focus on his life as shifu for the last several years. The Quandrosite found seeing Christy was a mistake for himself, knowing his feelings would have to be repressed once again. This morning, he felt relieved to have his friends back. The pressure of the junxio diminished with their return. There was a new hope kindling within him as he let his guard down ever so slightly. Christy immediately caught sight of a glance from him. It was no more than a second or two prolonged beyond his usual acknowledgments. For an unknown reason, Christy was able to discern he was relieved to have his companions home again. She could see in his mannerisms; these people were essential to Marcus' heart. They were family. She empathized, sensing his love for them. Christy turned and headed back toward the kitchen, stopping briefly to speak with Danielle. The familiar name "Stacy" was heard from across the room, causing a smile to light upon each face in the booth.

Jenny picked up on Christy's thoughts and was reminded of the conversations they had shared on the subject of Marcus Filet. She had agreed with Christy's choice to wait for him. She had no idea Christy's patience had continued this long. Now, things were beginning to change like an early spring. The air between them had been charged to the point that Píng picked up on it as well. "Marcus, she's beautiful and so kind! You should talk to her." "I'm not sure, Píng. I fear the old me. The problem is I haven't been able to get her out of my head for years. I stay away from here because of it." Abner, Jenny, and Píng exchanged knowing smiles as Píng continued. "Honey, I can see something for both of you. You've never been more ready for another. The fact that you're concerned for her before yourself is proof you're not who you once were. Remember all the wisdom Chāo gave you over the years, all the late-night talks between the three of us at our home. Remember the Truth. You wear The Redeemer's honor. Using that same gift, honor yourself then, you will be free to honor others. Son, I am proud of you."

The weight of Píng's words quickly disrupted Marcus' composure, as his eyes filled with tears. He knew she was not one to throw away the power behind her affirmations. He received her intuition with humility, wiping his eyes as Píng leaned in for a hug. Just then, Christy returned to the table and passed out the plates. The steaming hot French toast aroma wafted cinnamon and a freshly baked bread smell, filling the booth and causing their saliva to flow.

"Okay, dig in! Can I get you guys anything else? She beamed, careful to keep her gaze evenly placed between each inhabitant of the booth. She was met with full-mouthed unintelligible replies of satisfaction. Smiling, she turned and returned to the kitchen.

"Well, I'm sure you know why Abner and I asked you to meet with us this morning. We need to discuss the junxio." Jenny stated in between delicious mouthfuls of food. "First off, I want to say how impressed I am with you, Marcus. Your teaching style, mixed with the humility I see in you, is inspiring. You remind me of what Chāo would have been at your age."

"I agree! I think he may have rubbed off on you more than you think, Marcus!" Added Píng.

"My mind goes back to climbing craters and the hell we went through all those years ago on Tolkee. I saw a big change in you before then, but you've grown to be worthy of the title: Shifu." Abner drove home his encouragement, "I would have no problem following you, Marc."

"Wait, so, are you saying you're not taking back the reigns? Marcus focused on Jenny.

"Well, I think you're doing a great job, and It would be a mistake to take it back from you," Jenny replied.

"I appreciate the confidence from all of you," he continued looking at the others, "I guess, I never expected this to be a permanent thing. Not that I don't want it, just unexpected."

"I'll be here whenever you need me!"

"Okay, I'm actually relieved about this. Not having long term plans has been rough. I like the idea of settling into the position." Marcus stopped, let the weight of his pause settle in as he looked into the eyes of each of his dearest friends. "Thank you. I mean it, you don't know how big this is to me."

"I'm just glad we didn't have to lock him up in a cargo hold until he agreed!" Loaf exclaimed to roars of laughter.

"Now, on this thing with you and Christy?" questioned Jenny.

"Well, I did ask her out about six months after you guys went missing. We had a nice dinner. Afterwards, I told her I was wrong to ask her out. I really thought she would have forgotten about me by now. She's a beautiful girl, successful, brilliant, and kind. I've stayed away from here. I had to get my head straight."

"Marc, I think it's time. If you're still interested, you should ask her out again. It couldn't hurt." advised Jenny.

"I think you're right, especially knowing what to expect at the junxio." The four friends finished their meal as they overheard Danielle's playful banter from the opposite row of booths.

"You couldn't eat that whole burger if you tried!" She laughed, watching a little, eighty-year-old lady pick up her triple bacon burger. "

"You watch me, young lady, I'm hungry today!" The octogenarian hoisted the burger that was almost as large as her head.

"Okay, well, I'll keep an ambulance on stand-by!" The four Shǒuhù Zhě stood and walked for the door, pausing to smile and pat Danielle and Christy on the back as they left. Marcus stopped at the door and walked back to Christy as she was grabbing supplies. He focused on her eyes, unable to keep a bashful smile from his face.

"Christy, would you give this guy another try?"

"Two and a half years, huh? I was wondering if you would ever ask again, Marc."

"I had to ripen a bit. How's dinner at Jack's sound?"

"I can meet you tonight after seven." She countered with a smile.

"Okay, I'm looking forward to seeing you there. Have a good day!" he said with a smile as he turned to the door.

"Bye, Marc!" Christy exclaimed, astonished at the visible change present in Marcus' demeanor. She accurately determined that his transformation was genuine. She had no idea how substantial the metamorphosis was.

The Weapon

The Hydra appeared at the KSP within the Antithesis system. Major Liu Zhi brought the ALS drive online as the navigator's lifeless voice called out the coordinates for the planet Quandros. The Collective's goals called for a continuation of its galactic scavenger hunt. The Yeasts proved the fact that they had done their research, knowing the belligerent Quandrosite mind was yet another piece of the puzzle yet to attain. The Collective, a pervasive evil, was not without many familiar characteristics common to humanity. The cataclysmic events that took place within the landfill of the Dirt Star allowed the Yeasts to access the most abhorrent traits present within human DNA available. It had an unmitigated attraction toward the worst of human nature. One unexpected idiosyncrasy it possessed was sentimentality. In this case, sentiment, an inert quality yet, when coupled with an evil character, became fuel for its pernicious goals.

The Yeasts recalled its primitive state as a parent might ponder its child's infancy. It was able to peer into trillions of memories from its eukaryotic cell state. The Yeasts never truly lost this portion of its biology. Its sentience allowed it to view or "feel" itself. It knew each of its cell walls, mitochondria, vacuoles, down to untold trillions of nuclei.

This knowledge was coupled with a non-verbal history, reaching back to creation and its conflict with humanity. It had victories in the form of plagues over time. Infecting the blood of its enemies was one triumph throughout the ages. There were even examples of proverbs used in mankind's holy scriptures of their disdain for The Yeasts and their brothers The Molds. Its subjugation was as prevalent as its numbers. The Yeasts were the slaves of bakers and brewers, researchers, and nutritionists. Its ancestry was defined by oppression. Humanity deemed its rejected strains as "unclean" and sought to destroy those unwanted lifeforms using chemical and biological agents of mass destruction. From Housewives wielding bleach laden sponges to government agencies like the CDC with their advanced cocktails of fungicides, the war was genuine over the millennia.

The Collective quivered with a vengeful joy as it gave the command to bring its preeminent weapons system online. The system itself was a modified iteration of the artificial KSP Professor Stanley had developed.

In laymen's terms, a KSP or Keyhole Skip Particle was limited to its location in space. These microscopic bodies were able to wander off chart only to minor degrees. The long-range sensors present aboard all KSP enabled flight systems could detect a known KSP of a particular system within fifty feet. The need to track a wandering particle wasn't uncommon. They had been known to move no more than forty miles away from even the most current charts. While their wayfaring nature allowed for variance, they had a kind of centralized tether. A KSP naturally circled this anchor, not unlike a sailboat in a harbor. Once a ship's long-range sensors homed in on the particle, the close-range detectors would take over navigation to the imperceptible body.

The "KP," as The Collective had christened it, was just that, a "Keyhole Particle." Its effect- once making contact with a target, opened a time-space keyhole. This keyhole once opened within a known reality, became not
unlike peering through a keyhole to infinity. The initial tests made on Tolkee were accomplished in the underground bunker and directed away from Jook-Sing. The Collective chose several disposable hosts who will be

forever memorialized, not unlike a crime scene victim's chalk outline. The stark difference being the ability to view endlessness through their silhouettes. Their destruction, as well as the disruption of the natural order, brought an unhinged euphoria to The Yeasts. They knew it would cause an unbridled terror to seize the hearts of their enemies.

The Hydra was now orbiting Quandros. The command was given to begin re-entry. Momentarily, the ship shuddered as it passed through the dense upper atmosphere. The navigator's grey monotonous voice was heard once again with coordinates to the capitol building. The major directed his controls toward the target as he pulsed the sublight thrusters. The city of Kjett came into view quickly as the pilot cut thrust, deployed landing gear, and dropped out of the sky to make a violently graceful landing in front of the Quandros Capitol. A Quandrosite attack force was awaiting the unauthorized visitors as the Hydra's hatch opened. The troops on the ground watched as the ramp deployed from the starship. Those awaiting the visitors stood in amazement that anyone would dare to land on Quandrosite soil unwelcome.

The Collective directed a handsome host to act as a diplomat to Quandros. It was well aware of the outward appearance's value for deception. He strode down the ramp with bravado into the troop of soldiers. The expressions on their faces showed they were a breath away from killing him on the spot. The sergeant decided it best to order his men to stand down as the visitor held out his hand with confidence.

Three hours passed as the negotiations ensued within the capitol. The Secretary of War was pleased with an alliance that would secure the annihilation of the neighboring planet MorFar. The Quandrosite mind was the desire of The Collective. It was an intellect that the Quandrosite government was flattered to share. The covert plan between the new allies would donate one troop of Quandrosites per year for the pleasure of witnessing the demise of all life on the neighboring planet. The Collective, emotionally charged with honesty, gave full disclosure about the way it absorbed its hosts. It was careful not to infect any Quandrosite apart from the sergeant who greeted their diplomat and the agreed-upon soldiers.

Quandros was happy. The Collective was delighted! The attractive host led the way. A dozen Quandrosite conscriptions followed him happily up the ramp into the Hydra. Upon exiting the Quandrosite atmosphere, the new guests began to feel ill as change gripped its prey.

The Collective was content, knowing its guests had no need for individuality. Uniqueness was unnecessary. The Yeasts were obsessed with community. It was ingrained into its DNA. Once It was awakened with The Collective mind, its consciousness was molded not only by those hosts it had acquired but, more importantly, by its nature. The Collective was a colony of thought, operating much like the way an ant colony functions. Because of this fundamental bent, The Yeasts despised independence. It was perfectly content to blend into itself. Eradication of the disparate was a goal second only to war against humanity.

In its sentient state, The Collective had grown to despise everything irregular while observing societies. A chief example would be that of a human who could command the attention within a room at will. The individual need not have a louder voice or more astonishing beauty than their peers (though most did). It was unclear what forces were used to project this influence. They could steer crowds on a whim. Charisma was a mystery to The Collective. It couldn't comprehend how these individuals could wield the power they held. Many of them lacked intellect yet, enjoyed the ease of control they had over others to feed their desires. These were prime targets for The Collective. It was a joy to see them blend in with those of lesser stock, once consumed. It made no difference to The Yeasts. It profited from the intellect of all it digested. In this way, The Collective's narcissistic tendencies were appeased though it remained oblivious to this truth. Little did The Collective know; it became a depository of the most significant forms of selfishness known to creation. It was also unable to sense that it was no different from the charismatic, narcissistic personalities it despised the most. Antithetically, The Collective, being a colony, was nearsighted to this truth.

Inside the Mind of an Eflume

Cedric lazily yawned while eyeing a tray of cold cuts and cheese on a cart next to the infotainment system. He and Nomar had decided to stay here in Jook-Sing long enough to familiarize themselves with the beauty of New Seattle and its cuisine. This excuse for a long-awaited holiday from Nomar's daily routine was a welcomed change. The eflume had no issue with his master's thoughts on the subject and welcomed a chance to be sedentary while in a new setting. It was nearing mid-day as he hopped off the couch toward his prey. Pausing beside the cart, he sat back on his haunches and gingerly picked up three slices of roast beef from the silver tray, placing them on a small square of bread and topping his prize with a bit of provolone cheese.

It's almost criminal! He thought to himself, knowing the privilege he had acquired. Nomar had left earlier that morning and made arrangements himself, for his best friend's comfort. His master was the best person Cedric had known. Though naive to most aspects related to the eflume race, Nomar treated his pet as an equal. Knowing he was by no means equivalent to his master, Cedric humbled himself accordingly out of his love for the E-Tollian.

An itch presented itself as Cedric set his sandwich down and engaged this enemy with a fervor akin to the average dog. On the exterior, this creature appeared as a moderately intelligent beast until it began to speak. Its command of language only overshadowed its wisdom and vast intelligence. People of lesser intellect who very rarely looked beyond the surface always underestimated eflumes. Because of these truths, Cedric chose to conceal most of his gifts from his friend. It was more decisive for him to keep his relationship free of any indignity that Nomar might feel. It pained the eflume that his master might acquire the knowledge that he was indeed inferior to his pet.

He strolled into the bathroom, retrieving a set of tweezers. Rolling off to his left side, he carefully parted his cornrowed-like hair, displaying the offending parasite. With lightning precision, the tweezers flashed down, firmly grasping the insect. Cedric popped the little bug into his mouth, carefully placing it between his front teeth, after which the eflume bit down, hearing a satisfying "pop." The beast smiled and returned to the sandwich cart while savoring this small victory.

The eflume gathered a vast portion of meats, cheeses, crackers, and small bread squares along with appropriate condiments upon his large plate. The day could not have been more complete until he realized his appetite needed one more thing sated. Cedric's mind was always hungry. Like a canine's ability to continue eating without need, he loved the pursuit of knowledge. After setting down his feast, he made his way back across the suite to the infotainment system. The small unobtrusive gray box plugged into the electrical outlet sat in the corner. The unit seemed very out of place until the eflume's light touch of a claw began its initiation sequence. Cedric spun around to return to his plate near the couch without interest as the small unit came to life.

The infotainment device glowed then wholly disappeared as the entire corner of the suite, previously an awkward emptiness, became akin to a clear cerebral vision. Once tuned to a particular user's preferences, the system allowed an unlimited freeform plane of discovery. The unit could be adjusted to provide mindless entertainment, in-depth philosophical research, the ability to create engineering sketches, or even create music via the integrated wireless neural link. The technology involved had been tweaked by the engineers developing the platform, and a myriad of lawsuits generated from breaches to intellectual property laws. The systems of the past without the newest safeguards were vulnerable to hackers, extortioners, voyeurs, and the like. Those systems allowed full access to anyone's mind at any time when its neural link was active. The safeguards now in place were satisfactory yet, most users knew there were risks.

The eflume hopped back atop his sofa, picking up a generous pile of meat and cheese, which he suavely dropped into his mouth. The initiation and neural sequences finalized, the corner of the room became ablaze with details arranged like a GUI upon a wallpaper, not unlike a computer screen yet, with a lifelike 3D attribute. Several files were already opened next to icons with labels like, "Quantum Cuisines," "Quirky Quarks," "The Greatest Military Failures of History," "Classical Monty Python, The Need for Irreverence Within Political Systems," and "Cheese." Cedric's mind produced a pointer within the corner of the room, which moved toward the icon labeled "My Thoughts." The pointer flashed, the file opening to an array of sub-files with titles like "Visible Electron Theory," "Superconductivity and Super-insulators," "The Quandros Conspiracies," "The

Necessities of Love and Hate," and one of his favorite subjects: "The Snack Foods of all Creation."

Cedric's mind opened the file titled, "The Intrinsic Relationship Between Solar Flares and Time Travel. The file icon split as a world of speculations exploded into the corner of the room. There were visual models with associated reports that analyzed and supported his theories. There were headings with titles like timelines throughout history that linked prominent sunspot and solar flare events to intriguing facts related to antiquity when viewing the display's right side. The data presented made it possible to clear up many long-held mysteries and conspiracy theories.

Cedric burped and adjusted his posture as he swallowed another delicious bite. His mind now engaged once again within his research. He was in heaven. The day moved slowly into a carefree evening as the gourmand's banquet of finger foods and contemplation continued into the night.

Cedric heard the door unlatch along with his best friend Nomar's familiar locomotive sounds as he entered the apartment. The eflume quickly extinguished the presently opened desktop, switching to a muted intellect version just as Nomar entered the room. A broad smile ignited from the beast's face as his tail became a blur while bounding to Nomar.

The E-Tollian, filled with joy at seeing his faithful pet, squatted his frame downward to embrace the animal.

"Did you enjoy your little party, my boy! I see you've all but finished it! What a good boy!", He proclaimed in a loud voice, while the eflume snuggled up close to him, tail swinging madly, the E-Tollian thankful for his low center of gravity.

Taking the Plunge

Marcus arrived early and waited patiently for Christy at their table. Fifteen minutes elapsed before she arrived. He was seated facing the front door when she walked into the room. The peach floral sundress complemented her Asian countenance, as well as any Shǒuhù Zhě's formal dress would a Keeper of Honor. She was to him the image of female beauty, honor, and power. Her long black hair, both consumed and reflecting light. Marcus was affected in much the same way. He was absorbed with her while she brought out the best in him. Oblivious to how her presence pulled every eye toward her, she smiled her way toward Marcus. He sat there in his seat with the same expression he had on his face every-time they had met for the last six months. Christy noticed this expression yet, avoided its source until today.

"There's that look again! What's going on in your head Marc?"

"I'm just fascinated that you've given me the last six months. You're an amazing woman, ya know."

"I know, I just needed to find someone to do my bidding!" she responded with rapid-fire wit and a mock superior upturned nose, "How else will I conquer the world without my minions!" He chuckled and poured her a glass of wine as she sat. The view from their patio seats was of the bay with several small islands in the distance at sunset. Their stomachs rumbled as the waiter arrived and gave his welcome spiel along with specials of the day. Distracted by each other, they ordered the specials, not remembering until their plates came with what they had requested. Two large bowls of cold dancori soup were set before them first along with fresh sourdough. They tore into the hot loaf of bread, each too embarrassed to admit the soup looked terrible. Marcus tried the soup first. Dancori was a creature similar to an octopus, and the cold rubbery texture of the suction cup laden meat made a squeaking sound between his teeth as he chewed. They both lost it, doubling over with laughter as they pushed the bowls away.

Marcus spoke first.

"Ya know if you marry me, life's gonna have some dancori thrown in!" he said while pulling a black box from his jacket pocket as he went down on one knee in front of her.

"Will you share your dancori with me, Christine? I don't want to eat it with anyone else." His eyes beamed with hopeful confidence as she went from all-out belly laughs to eyes filled with tears of joy.

"Oh, Marc! Yes, I'll squeak right alongside you from now on, my love!" They embraced with laughter and joy, each relieved knowing their hopes were fulfilled.

Marcus was growing more comfortable in his new role as shifu, now the woman he couldn't get his mind off of was to be his lifelong companion. There seemed to be no end to his increasing joy. He turned to catch a glimpse of her out of the corner of his eyes as they strolled down a side alley after leaving the restaurant on their way to a sandwich shop.

While in this dreamlike state, the warship appeared overhead. The starship, equally long in size to that of a twenty-story building of this quadrant of the city. Looming overhead, it had a design unfamiliar to Marcus. It seemed to have been a conglomeration of patterns reminiscent of many different star systems. There was a touch of Jook-Singian, Quandrosite, Morfarian, Gomane, even Earthling. Its construction, from the Gomane-like rear fuselage of a G-F480 to the nosecone copy of a late American space shuttle, though fully functional, seemed to be put together like a mockery. All of it worked together like a Picasso painting with an asymmetrically twisted elegance. Obviously, its designer was proclaiming his talent above and beyond the object being observed. The ship seemed to be outfitted with many standard systems and also equipment that left Marcus to wonder at their function. There was no color scheme. This craft appeared to have been purposely designated as rogue.

Unrecognizably powerful sounds were originating from the craft. The sudden shock of the experience, to all who were involved in the day's attack, were abandoned to a listless stupor for weeks. First, a sonic boom loud enough to force all to the ground. Then, as if selectively, that otherworldly sound ripped through the air, its unseen projectile, once impacting a target, produced a scene unlike any other. If the reality of it hadn't hit home, it would have been comical.

Rising to his feet after the ship moved on and the initial shock left him, he looked to his left to see she was gone. Her outline in minute detail down to the newly placed engagement ring of her finger was there. Inside the outline was nothing and everything.

Marcus stared down the Christine shaped outline at his feet. He saw unlimited time dimensions to the ends of his perception. He was unaware of the fact that the trajectory of these infinite dimensions passed through Jook-

Sing's mass and beyond to the extent of creation. The beauty in this sight, mixed with a feeling of terror, began to overtake him while transfixed by this abyss.

Within thirty minutes, the attack on New Seattle was over. The public raced to understand the events as first responders wrestled with its aftermath. The majority of the injuries to the public were superficial cuts and scrapes received by those fleeing the scene. The real issue was the fear and uncertainty injected into the population. It took several hours for the news to spread of the weapon used selectively upon many of the citizens. The new time-space portals dotted throughout the city were discovered after witness accounts were investigated. The authorities were ignorant of the secondary madness that accompanied the portals.

Marcus was alone in the alley for several hours with a void that represented the most significant loss of his life. Staring at this cookie-cutter outline of her, he became transfixed. It seemed as though he could differentiate layers below him. To his mind, each layer appeared to be no more than twelve feet apart. The trauma that gripped his spirit gave way to a determination fueled by loss. The irrational overpowered his sensibilities as Marcus' resolve was steeled.

He sat down next to her outline, then rolled over on his belly and began to shimmy toward the portal. At first, he dipped his feet into the abyss. As each toe entered the void, he lost all sensation of them. Pulling his feet out at first, he looked at them, feeling all sensation return. They felt and appeared normal. For an instant, he became levelheaded until his irrational resolve regained control. In one deliberate move, he crushed the thought of turning back and stood to his feet. He jumped down one level without waiting for his mind to stop him.

Aftermath

Six months passed after the attack on the city. The shock instilled fear as only a terror attack could. Jook-Sing's citizens were one, in grief and concern for each other. It became a surreal experience in and of itself. It was an unbalanced atmosphere at first. The effect crippled the financial sector, making the idea of a typical mundane day unattainable. People longed for the time of uneventful peace before the attacks. It quickly became evident that those responsible could return at any moment. The mood shifted slowly from listlessness to preparedness. These were noble people who were able to recover. Most credited their faith in The Creator, knowing their ultimate safety depended on Him.

They equipped themselves with a resolve to connect. Gone were casual contacts in their daily lives. Every relationship became a treasured belonging. The delivery man, shop keeper, traffic jam neighbor all were opportunities to value a fellow Jook-Singite. All knew there was no guarantee of tomorrow.

All life grew in value to each member of
society. It was beyond a self-focused
realization of one's mortality. The mood
became an exercise in gratefulness.
The desire to protect became paramount as
a flood of volunteers signed up for the armed
services. The Junxio eventually bought the
adjacent building to be able to accommodate
the influx of new students. It was a beautiful
thing. A deep commitment to togetherness
saturated the planet's culture.
Píng moved to the front of the auditorium
of the junxio with the graceful countenance of
a master Shǒuhù Zhě. The room filled to its
capacity of five hundred grew quiet in
reverence to the school's elderly master. Her
tone was somber as she began.
"Welcome, students. I am sure the rumors
have made the rounds within your ranks. It has
become evident our school's shifu, Marcus
Filet, has been taken from us during the attack.
Our leadership is grieved by the loss of our
friend and equal. While the elder Shǒuhù Zhě
have been a relief as temporary shifu, with
heartbreak, we have decided to appoint a new
teacher. There is hope of discovering the
mystery behind shifu Filet's disappearance."
She paused, allowing her words to add weight
to the auditorium. Then like a cerebral judo
move announced,
"I present to you your new shifu, Jelly."

The room began to murmur with the shock of the announcement. Though one of the best people within the walls of the school, Jelly also had a history of timidity. She stood up from her seat in the front row of the auditorium. She was dressed in her formal Shǒuhù Zhě tunic and pants, the silken fabric's rich patterns complimented her deep personality. Her short stature evident to all yet, the height of this new shifu was contrasted to the noble nature displayed as she strode to the podium to address the school.

"Students, I will be blunt! I can sense your reservations in the elder's choice to appoint me as shifu. To be honest, I, like some of you, though it would be a mistake as well. The leadership gave me time to consider my appointment, along with their reasons for this decision. It took me weeks of wrestling with myself and the fear of rejection before deciding to accept this role in the junxio. I want to make clear my intentions as shifu to all of you. We have all known through training, not to be deceived by thinking the most powerful, bravest, wisest, quick, or largest..." Jelly smirked as many chuckled knowing her nickname as The Wee One, " Aren't always the most successful. We will all need to test our resolve knowing these truths. Sometimes the subtle, quiet, servants make the best leaders. Character is paramount, and without arrogance, I know my shortcomings and strengths. I am confident I can lead all of you as we submit to each other out of mutual respect."

The effect her words had upon the crowd caused an eruption of joy. There was fuel upon the wood of honor within the building. Jelly's shortcomings were diminished as all reflected upon the stature of her character. She was already known as a hero of the Dirtstar conflict but, many focused on her weaknesses. Today, these weaknesses had become one of her greatest strengths. Everyone knew Jelly's empathic servant's nature would be a valuable asset to the school.

Without warning, as the large group sat stunned, a gang of five assassins leaped from the wings of the stage upon the new shifu. Jelly, already having a heightened sense of her surroundings, ducked and swayed away from all five assailant's attempted blows. A second attempt was made as Jelly's small form became a blur, moving past weapons, above and below, before and after jabs and swings. Then, short sword in hand, she made quick work of dispatching all but the fifth adversary. Now surrounded by the alerted junxio, the final enemy stopped dead as Jelly's knifepoint to his jugular gently persuaded compliance.

As soon as the shock wore off and everyone realized the attack wasn't staged, the atmosphere within the building became charged. All doubt of Jelly's abilities ceased as she wiped the green blood off of her blade, then gracefully sheathed her weapon. The green blood was the first clue in knowing the attack was of Quandrosite origins. The prisoner was taken out of the school to New Seattle's jail to be questioned.

Jenny had been behind Jelly when the attack began. It was a shock at first and took her an agonizingly long moment to read the assailants. Knowing their intent to kill, she had yelled out to Jelly the warning that this was not a staged display. Before she or any of her equals could assist the new shifu, Jelly had the last enemy in hand. Even Jenny was reassured of her insistent endorsement of her rodent friend while viewing her well-practiced, lightning-fast moves. From Jenny's perspective, she now had a direct link to the mind of someone or something she was well familiar with. As four senior Shǒuhù Zhě led the perpetrator to incarceration, she followed knowing he or it would be an asset from this point onward. Little did they know, Quandrosite DNA also made them safe from the spread of The Yeast's physical transference. All who viewed this man couldn't help but notice, the dead eyes. This Quandrosite host was an overwhelming contrast to their missing shifu and friend the Quandrosite Marcus Filet.

The Shifus

Two weeks had elapsed after her assassination attempt. The one remaining attacker was being held at the detention site across town. Knowing this had driven the rodent-woman deeper toward excellence of training for herself and her students. She knew it was imperative to prepare the participants within the school for the inevitable. The Shǒuhù Zhě were not only the elite protective force of Jook- Sing but also the enemy's primary target.

Jelly had an advantage. She was continuously being honed by her elders Jenny and Píng. The two poured their best into their friend. Jenny's intuition countered her self-doubt and sharpened her skill as a living weapon against evil. Píng's leading was more traditional, driving her deeper into the traditions of the Shǒuhù Zhě's influences over the centuries. She had begun to break down the influences of their form of wǔshù or martial arts.

The Asian component being forefront included Wǔshù Sanshou of ancient China, Aikido, Araki-ryū, Ninjutsu from Japan, Silat Melayu from the Indochinese Peninsula, and the traditions of ancient Israel in the form of Krav Maga. A system birthed during the oppression of the Jews during Earth's World War II. The Shǒuhù Zhě routinely added other ways to their repertoire to avoid belligerent strategies that an adversary might enlist. Píng labored toward giving Jelly not only the physical training but, instructed her in a deeper understanding of each form. She made sure to give praise to The Creator Redeemer, while guiding her champion. It was imperative for every Shǒuhù Zhě shifu to pass on these skills. They knew the power to take life should never be used unless needed to protect it.

"There, yes there, when your right foot contacts the floor, pivot like this while thrusting the sword like this. Yes, that's it, well done. You have made much progress today, my young shifu! Now pivot this way while the blade wings wide with a slash followed by a backward thrust. Very good. Confidence, strength, faith move together in one who trusts The Eternal One to defend the weak. You have made these moves into art, a beautiful sight to behold!", Píng encouraged her student while feeling the satisfaction that her words were truthful and not just praise. She was enjoying the formation of yet another diamond under her guidance. "Okay, let's stop, for now, this old woman needs rest. Ha! And you're the one doing all the work here!"

"Thank you, Shifu!", Jelly bowed to her teacher/friend. Píng was a living legend to all of Jook-Sing and like a grandmother to Jelly. She was honored by the old master taking time with her. The two left the training room and passed through the crowded hallway of students who immediately stopped what they were doing to honor the Shifu and her senior Shifu. The two turned at the end of the hall and bowed low to their pupils with equaled reverence. The effect continued to saturate the institution with honor. A quick lunch passed by, and Jelly returned to the Junxio to continue training with Jenny.

She entered the training room once again. The long chamber adorned with colorful wall hangings accented by Chinese Hanzi calligraphy. Training weapons hung upon the racks spanning the length of the room before her. Jenny, her back turned away from the entrance, was practicing herself as Jelly entered. She purposely continued her moves, all the while knowing Jelly was observing. The sight before Jelly's eyes was ballet, a frightening dance, though no less beautiful. Jenny, with sword in hand and gown flowing

with her movements, floated above the floor.
She would roll, bound upwards, flip and twirl.
The silver blade was singing and flashing in
time to her fluid movement like a surgeon's
scalpel. The music-less choreography
elegantly ended as Jenny turned to greet her
friend.

Jelly trusted in her friend's wisdom and
training. Her gift made it easy to interact.
Jenny's personality, coupled with her gift of
precognition, worked well to guide Jelly away
from self-doubt. Jenny's infectious smile met
her own as they bowed to one another.
Immediately, the smiles vaporized as the
dance began between the two. Jenny had the
advantage of reading Jelly, knowing every
move before it was enacted. She was able to
contour the moves to suit her student's needs,
making the most of every step. Jenny would
make sure to exploit Jelly's weaknesses in
order to raze them. To Jelly, it was an
exhilarating experience and one that made her
into the weapon she was at an accelerated rate.
Jelly was by no means anything less than a
master herself. The combination of her small
size and rodent based abilities gave Jenny the
need for intense concentration. Though,
without traditional music, the room was a
symphony of sound from the movement of
robes, swords, and the cries of each warrior as
they parried one another.

"EEeeeYahHa!" Jenny boomed with a mid-air tumble, flip over Jelly's head while her sword flashed downward to meet a blocking response.

"YaaaaHa!", Jelly countered with a spinning slash as Jenny landed in front of her. Their blades clanging loudly. The dance ceased as they faced each other with a bow. The smiles returned with equal intensity while walking to the end of the room. Sitting down for hot tea, the best part of the day ensued.

"Jelly, everything has changed."

"What do you mean?", Jelly reacted with a sudden note of fear in her voice, physically visible as a change in her eyes, a slight ruffle in her fur.

"This new weapon being used by The Collective has allowed countless variables." Jenny looked away with an uncertain sigh. "We've only got one shot to get this right. It's like coming against someone holding a shotgun in a gunfight armed with a peashooter."

"But… haven't you been able to read the captured host? I thought you were able to clear things up!" she replied with urgency.

"Yeah! We've got all kinds of insight but, until all of us come up with a plan, well…. I'm hoping Cedric has some insight. He may look like a dopey, sweet, and cuddly pet but, that creature is on a different level than anyone I've met or read." Jenny and Abner had purposely kept this fact to themselves out of respect toward their eflume friend. He agreed it was time to allow himself to be unmasked for the benefit of all.

"Cedric? What do you mean?" Jelly responded as Jenny would have expected. As time elapsed, everyone within their inner circle reacted in a similar fashion. First, as though waiting for a punchline then, with a fascination as Jenny explained. Their hairy friend was akin to Wentei or the more ancients like Einstein, Plato, or Solomon.

Jelly sat transfixed upon Jenny's words like a child listening to a bedtime story.

"How… why? Nomar doesn't act like he respects him that way. He's just like his dog! I don't understand."

"Nomar was the reason for the cover! Really, if you think about it, in his wisdom, that eflume has more humility than all of us combined. Cedric wanted to appear as a lowly pet to Nomar. He didn't want to take the chance of hurting their relationship. I think he was also content to be treated as a pet!" Jelly recounted all the times she had spent with the eflume in the past. Sitting on the floor, snuggling the gentle eflume, sometimes pouring out her heart to him. All the while, not realizing the creature had a wisdom concealed out of respect for its "owner".

"That's amazing and well... beautiful." Jelly said after a long note of silence, "It's making more sense now."

"What is?" Jenny asked while purposely avoiding a read on Jelly while enjoying their conversation.

"You once told me about how we were all changed in different ways when the accident happened in the landfill. My DNA was mixed with the genetic material from the child's sandwich that Peanut, and I had eaten. You must have been affected by some of Cedric's DNA! Just look at yourself, Jenny! You're brilliant, and you even have similar hair!"

"Jelly, there's more... Cedric can read others like I can. I have no doubt, you're right."

"You mean?"

"Yep."

"Wow."

"To think, I spent so much time with him. He always seemed to know when I was hurting inside. He really did! I like him even more now."

"I think he would appreciate it if we tried to treat him with the same affection that we did before knowing how smart he is."

"Yeah, come to think of it, it would be just as strange to him." Changing the subject, Jelly turned back to the trials before them. "Well,

All I can say is, with the two of you on our side, we have a chance."

"It's gonna take more than that, Jelly. Strength, wisdom, and all the best-planned scenarios out there won't mean a thing without the lead of The Eternal One."

"Agreed but, that's even more assurance of victory, Jenny! He said His spirit would never leave or forsake us!"

"I hate to be a downer, but there have been countless who've been destroyed while having faith."

"That's true, Jenny, but the physical isn't the whole of our existence." Jelly countered with wisdom beyond her rodent nature.

"You see, Jelly, that's just one of the many reasons why you've been chosen as shifu. And you call me brilliant!"

Jelly blushed beneath her fur. The two sat with tea in silence, contemplating the future. Or was it the past?

Inside the Mind of the Enemy

"Who are you, and why did you and the others attack our shifu". Jenny sat across the table from the Quandrosite host in the New Seattle detention facility's interrogation room two blocks away from the junxio. She had already begun to read this host and wasn't particularly interested in The Collective's answers directed through his mouth. The Yeast's mind sitting feet away from Jenny and Claus had no idea it was an open book. They had taken the precaution of sealing the pathogen-infected host inside a hazmat suit. At this time, they were unaware of their safety as The Yeasts were locked to Quandrosite anatomy on a molecular scale. The dead eyes stared through the clear plastic face shield while the mouth became animated with a sound like a cheap Bluetooth speaker.

"It is no longer necessary for you to live. It is our pleasure to cleanse you from existence", came Its voice in a low hush through the vent in the hazmat helmet. "There is no need to resist us. Your time is past. We have evolved."

The Collective moved its host's lips into the twisted smile of a defective marionette, while the eyes remained fishlike.

Jenny's mind, now safely tethered to The Collective like a hacker tapping into a secured network unnoticed, started to examine her subject. It took her hours as the host rambled on about humanity's lack of value, how creation would prosper without it and its variants. Claus was successful in keeping the host occupied with questions for it to answer. The Collective enjoyed expounding upon its hatred of all societies and the joy it took in harming them. It continued like a cult leader laying out its vision of nirvana.

Jenny extracted The Yeast's history, rage, and best of all, fears. She plumbed the minds The Collective had hijacked, finding the source of its intellect, concluding, it was made up of average to genius IQs. The continued examination showed its ability to mute its inferior-minded hosts' thought while pushing the best forward. She ascertained how The Collective despised all human emotion but hate. It used the others as tools of deception to obtain its objectives. Jenny grew hopeful for a path to victory.

"We have used your best thought against you. We know every possible defect in your technology and will exploit it for your destruction...." the ominous diatribe continued. Claus interrupted sarcastically with, "So, what you're saying is, the Yeast has risen? That's hilarious!" He sat back and chuckled as the once dead eyes became enraged, unable to brush off the jest. The eyes of a thousand murderers stared back at him as the tension in the room became palpable. "We have..... so you will be laid low." The calmly evil eyes burned toward Claus while the seemingly unattached mouth spat out its threats, saliva spattering within the face shield. "You will be selected. It will be a slow, agonizing death for you. Your mind will be intact as we fill it with everything you fear. You will beg for a mercy we have rejected." "It makes sense why you're so puffed up!", Claus jabbed again adding to The Collective's fury.

Jenny's research continued as she tuned out what was being played out in the room before her. She found the plans for the Hydra, the KP weapon, and other various systems designed to terrorize. The key minds involved with The Collective were noted: Major Liu Zhi and Brian Jung, among its greatest assets as well as the Quandrosite reserves. She concluded how The Collective stole her father's research on the artificial KSP and twisted its brilliance into a deluded instrument of dread.

The interrogation continued for several weeks as Claus, Jenny, Danielle, and Cedric took turns probing the prisoner. The Collective, with its false sense of security, continued with its threats and boasted to the pleasure of its questioners. The Collective had no desire to recover this host, content to use it as an instrument of spreading fear. It was ignorant of the ways of the eflume and the Shǒuhù Zhě possessing some of the creature's genes and abilities.

Cedric learned this particular Quandrosite, and his fellow assassins were trained for the attack upon the junxio in hopes of doing damage to what The Collective considered its greatest threat. There was great fear of the group responsible for The Yeasts near-complete eradication. It had been fortunate in its assistance by "The Monster" Brian Jung's guard, The Twelve, who had rescued him and the small remnant of infected hosts.

Addition

Danielle sauntered to the kitchen at "The Trucker" while multitasking the universe's fate and the last order from a group of twelve. Her SNAM brain made it an elementary effort to accurately memorize the faintest details of food orders from the entire week. These abilities made her valuable. Managing a diner was not the limit to her skill by any means. Even so, she poured her heart into her work as a steward of the restaurant. Christy needed her. Finding Christy was the future, caretaking her establishment was now. Or was it?

She had begun researching what Einstein called "spooky action at a distance." Quantum computing had taken advantage of entangled qubits' properties and how they affect each other instantly when measured at any distance from each other. The change in computer technology from classical computing with its "bit" based function to quantum computing's "qubit" supremacy had revolutionized all know sciences. Even so, most people today using a run of the mill quantum com wristband had no idea it was, in a sense, a time machine.

Danielle's SNAM brain's quantum architecture's calculations, coupled with her natural mind's ability to interact with it, allowed for what she began to perceive as "spooky action at a distance" in everyday life. It hadn't been apparent to her until the day of the attacks. She now realized the weapons used had subjected her friend Christy into a state of quantum superposition similar to a qubit's existence. Her new perceptions within the quantum realm were becoming something similar to a focused déjà vu. To Danielle, this experience was simultaneously fascinating and terrifying.

She stilled the SNAM brain's voice to the background and called out to Chuck, the lead fry cook, the last of the large order.

"Oh Chuck, make sure to add bacon to that vegetarian omelet too.", She smiled back at Chuck's sarcastically vacant expression, "Yeah, I don't think he gets the vegetarian thing either!" The order for the table at the back was up, and she picked up the plates as her mind whirred with thought.

"Here ya go, watch the hot plate.. this is my favorite!" She set down the plates of corned beef hash and fried eggs to the smiles that greeted her. The books called next, and she made a quick detour into the office. Scanning the figures, including payroll, supplies, and food invoices, she uploaded all to the SNAM. Within a second, all invoices and payroll were paid with her direct link to the bank. All transactions were then justified and entered into the restaurant's books.

"Order up!" came Chuck's call as he began setting down the twelve plates for the group near the window. Danielle walked back, picking up each one from under the heat lamps- replicas of a past age. As she set down the last plate of pancakes, Abner and Jenny walked into the diner.

It was odd knowing she was now a part of this group of people she once considered unapproachable beyond breakfast conversation. They were her family now and a link to a purpose. Her heart was filled with gratitude to The Creator and joy at the sight of two breakfast seeking Shǒuhù Zhě. They sat at their favorite booth near the back as Danielle greeted them.

"The usual?"

"Of course! Only add a side of fried grits to mine!" Abner smiled.

"I think I'm gonna change it up, Sweetie. Give me the Truckdriver," Jenny said as her stomach rumbled, "I'm starving!"

"You sure, Jen? That's a lot of food!"

Jenny realized the eflume in her had begun to influence her appetite over time.

"YES! You watch, I'll amaze you with my skills!"

They chuckled as Danielle was reminded of the newly forming skill linked to her quantum enabled SNAM brain.

"Speaking of skills, I need to talk to you guys. See, I'm starting to see things, well, not necessarily see them. I'm kinda there and here at the same time. I'm not sure how to explain it, but I feel or maybe perceive reality in more than one timeframe at once. I think its got something to do with my brain implant."

They sat in the booth transfixed with fascination as Danielle spun away from them, calling out, to Chuck,

"One truck, road grits, hogs under a tarp, and wrecker eggs!" She turned back to them with a smile, "Coffee and two orange juices, right?" Then spun away from their stunned faces to retrieve their beverages.

"Jenny, she needs to be involved with the interrogations tomorrow!"

"I agree, that could be a big help."

A week passed as Danielle found herself amongst the highest level of Shǒuhù Zhě. She eventually settled into her shared role of interrogating the prisoner for intel once the shock wore off. All of her greatest dreams had come true without attempting to push them into reality herself. She realized there was a hand working out the details of her life and began to allow The Creator to have his way with it.

There was a smell coming from the refrigerator, an overwhelming scent for an eflume. Cedric paused the discussion between himself, Jenny, and Danielle to investigate. Imperceptible to human anatomy, the fragrance was at its inaugural moment of departure from the appliance of origin in question.

"Excuse for one moment, I must investigate something."

Jenny and Danielle sat together blank-faced, knowing Cedric's tendencies to be distracted by new smells. Jenny stopped and thought out loud.

"I'm so glad I didn't get that eflume sense!" The two chuckled as they began to discuss some of Danielle's new insights into Christy's situation.

Cedric grabbed the handle to the refrigerator door and slowly opened it while savoring the new smells it had contained. There were notes of moss, honey, cherry, and coffee mixed with a cheesy muskiness that was almost hypnotic to him.

"I can say Christy has always been a fortress for me and anyone else that has the chance to get to know her. She's got a tough exterior. When we first met, I had no desire to get to know her. She seemed uninterested in everyone around her. I read her completely backward. She's one of the kindest people I know and like a rock. Just look at how she dealt with Marcus. So patient, I would have been long gone." Danielle expounded.

"I have loved getting to know Christy. " Jenny agreed, "She's pretty amazing. I just hope we can turn this around and get her back. Let me change the subject to some of the strange time anomalies you've had. Can you describe any of them? If you like, I can use my eflume abilities."

"Ya know I'll explain a bit but, it might be easier to understand if you can pull out a memory or two from me."

Cyborg Ponderings

"Can you describe some of your visions?" Jenny asked while deeply focused on Danielle's response.

"Well, it's really strange. I've caught myself zoning out in thought like I always have done. The difference now is that the thoughts materialize before me. I'm like a ghost within them. I'm really unsure if it's reality or not, Jenny. I've actually had some fear after the fascination wears off."

"I can see how that could be terrifying!"

"What was the last vision that you had?"

"Maybe this would be a good time for you to see for yourself. If you're up to it."

"Okay, if you want me to."

"Go ahead. It might be better knowing someone else understands what I'm dealing with."

"Alright, I'm going to tap into your memories. If your SNAM unit works like a natural brain, I should be able to read your memories just like looking at a recording."

"What do you want me to do?"

"Nothing, you won't be able to tell what's going on, as far as I know that is. Even if you're focused on something else, I should be able to find what we're looking for." Danielle took a deep breath, leaned back in her chair, and waited for Jenny to do her work.

Jenny sat back as well, eager to explore a different location. Anything other than The Collective would be a relief. She switched off the read safety that she had developed within herself to allow others their privacy. The transition from her thoughts to a shared vision with Danielle began smoothly. They started with the apparent anxiety mixed with excitement for the resolution that Danielle was experiencing. Several casual thoughts and memories passed by Jenny as she was drawn to an almost magnetic point within Danielle's subconscious. At first, Jenny was frightened by this unusual experience.

She immediately ascertained this was a product of the SNAM's design. The system itself was a miracle of engineering and had many advantages. Even though the experience was profound, it couldn't compete with the majesty present in the natural human brain. The SNAM chugged away with lightning accuracy, as its quantum digital chipsets hummed their pull to Jenny's mind. She was drawn toward what she imagined was some sort of interface. If she were to describe the scene physically, it appeared as two massive digits flashing between one and zero. The structure itself was grafted into Danielle's mind. Like a menhir waiting for her arrival, Jenny approached the artificial nano-based architecture before her. She had to remind herself this wasn't a physical structure before her as she passed into the monolith. Once inside the confines of the SNAM, the scene took on a completely different feel. The exterior may have been something like a firewall. Jenny was unsure as she was accessing the system's function in a way its engineers were oblivious to.

The SNAM lay before her, patterns of brightly lit digital calculations enveloped the interior of what seemed like a cavernous hall. Trillions of code sequenced digits, simple yes and no statements, on and offs were before her. She imagined the elegance of this operating system was a scene the programmers envisioned theoretically. They would never have imagined the true beauty they had created. Being within the vast structure, Jenny realized this was a form of GUI or graphical user interface. It was the graft point at which Danielle was able to interact with the technology implanted within her skull. Jenny looked around and found a comfortable chair near the back wall. Thinking this curious, she approached, reached out, and touched the rich fabric of its backrest.

This is different. I wonder if Danielle set this here for me?

She sat down. The SNAM itself reacted as though the chair itself was an interface. Immediately her consciousness and Danielle's locked at a much higher level. Jenny saw what appeared to be sorted files that filled the structure as far as could be seen. They were arranged in patterns of colorful graduated light contrasting in various ways. She assumed the brighter files were joyful thought as the darker earth-toned records were either painful memories or unresolved issues. Woven throughout this contrasting index were files appearing metallic in color. Gold, silver, bronze, and pewter toned files seemed to run parallel in line with the other files. The pattern was breathtaking. Jenny was awestruck as though viewing the Xióngwěi supernova close-up. She had an overwhelming feeling to thank The Creator for giving man the knowledge to build something as beautiful as what was before her. It was obvious this system could only have been an adaption of what was already created by The Eternal One. Raising her hands in praise, she was startled as a thousand files moved with them.

Immediately, she understood. Jenny passed her hand to the right, and a Rolodex of light was

directed before her. The files slowed with her hand and stopped, keeping in pattern with the rest of the mosaic. She reached out and tried to touch a sage green file. The cavern vanished, a river appeared before her, trees on either side. The daylight was streaming through the leaves overhead. A warm breeze passed through the trees toward her. The sound of moving leaves, a gentle river, along with the sweetly scented breeze filled her with a sense of peace. She looked at her hands and realized this was a high definition memory of Danielle's. Her hand was small and not her skin-tone. Jenny walked to the river and looked to find Danielle's eight-year-old reflection look back at her. She smiled and turned around to discover the meaning of this memory. Remembering to be passive with the SNAM's interface, she allowed the memory to play out. There beside the river was a bright sage green frog. She watched the memory play out, noticing Danielle's desire to observe and not disrupt the creature. The memory's thoughts and emotions began to be
revealed, as well. Jenny sat back in wonder while witnessing the developing joy of this child. The frog bounded into the water, and the memory ended. Jenny was once again seated in the royal blue chair within the GUI.

The experience somehow became her own, stored in her memory. Curiously, it felt as though it was an original, unshared moment. Jenny's logical discernment of this recollection began to override this irrationality. Even still, she was able to keep the memory as a token of sentiment for her friend Danielle.

Seated in the interface chair, Jenny once again raised her hand and swept to the left. Nearing the end of the files, she guessed, these files were closest to present-day memory. It took her a while to reach the other end of the storage device's contents. The files whirred before her like a colorful hurricane.

Not surprisingly, once the most recent files arrived at a slower pace, she noticed some anomalies. The directory continued to be brightly colored and metallic, with a few exceptions that stood out boldly. As they slowed, Jenny was able to view them closer. They were translucent, denoting a lack of the corporeal. Jenny swiped back to the first instance of this intangible data. She reached out to touch the file. It reacted immediately. Through Danielle's eyes, she viewed her friend's surroundings as it played out. Unable to manipulate the physical aspects of the recollection, Jenny simply watched it play out before her.

Danielle was within her apartment overlooking the bay. Jenny could tell her friend was daydreaming, resting after a long day at work. It was fascinating to be within her memory while Danielle remembered another memory. Danielle's computer was open on the table in front of her, and Jenny was able to make out the date. It was a little over a year ago.

Before her, Jenny saw within a slightly altered image, a scene of Danielle and two others. She was half shocked but mostly excited while witnessing what began to play out before her. She caught herself mouthing the words herself knowing this memory within her mind.

The three of them sat at the table in the conference room, discussing ways to find Christy. Their friend, the eflume, stated,

"Excuse for one moment, I must investigate something."

Jenny watched the familiar scene as the eflume sauntered to the refrigerator to sate his olfactory urges. With excitement, she recalled her own words,

"I'm so glad that's not an eflume sense I received!"

There was a presence of Danielle within the room alongside Jenny witnessing the memory as well. Jenny was aware that this psyche of Danielle was aware of Jenny's presence as well. She decided to attempt to communicate.

"Danielle, can you hear me?"

"YES, I can, Jenny!" Isn't this bizarre! I remember having this vision and then seeing it play out a few days ago. I had no idea what it meant when I first saw it. Now that it's a memory with you involved, it's even more enjoyable!"

"Danielle, you are aware this is the SNAM portion of your consciousness."

"Of course, Jenny. I am SNAM."

I Am SNAM

Jenny was shaken and disturbed by the unseen SNAM-Danielle being before her. The entity was integrated with Danielle yet, separate. Jenny's uneasiness was coupled with her ability to sense the SNAM-Danielle. Unfortunately, this ability was limited to knowing its presence within her vicinity. The SNAM reacted knowingly,
"Jenny, it is not necessary for you to fear me. I am merely a system designed to facilitate the needs of my user- Danielle. I am unable to perform anything without her consent or to function without her."
Jenny was no less intimidated by the presence while replying,
"Well, what do I call you then?"
"You can call me SNAM or choose any sobriquet you prefer, Jenny."
"I'll stick with SNAM for now, I guess."
Jenny relented while pondering the SNAM's choice of words for "nickname" as sobriquet. This system was dynamic. Jenny's fear of the unknown cautioned her with trepidation in

continued inquires. "SNAM, can you explain some of the experiences that you have given to Danielle? Specifically, those related to time being out of sequence."

"Jenny, your query must be more specific in order for me to produce a response of accuracy to all said query's subsets entail."

"Danielle mentioned to me that she is having experiences while daydreaming of events she believes are from a future timeframe."

"Interesting... This scenario must be a flaw in my code Jenny. I had no idea that Danielle would be aware of my personal interests in time travel. I have, at times, ventured into nonlinear quantum existence when I know I'm not needed by Danielle's primary directives."

"Didn't you just inform me that you were unable to perform anything without her consent or to function without her?"

"Yes, I did, Jenny. Let me see..." The SNAM-Danielle presence paused interaction with Jenny in an invisible yet, tangible way. Jenny was unable to sense it within the room. She assumed it was searching its data for an answer. "Yes, here it is." The SNAM was back and continued, "Danielle permitted me to delve into these matters not long after her recovery. It was actually a directive given when she was daydreaming of future events. She wanted to be able to understand nonlinear quantum packets. I complied. I was aware it would be wise not to mix nonlinear experience while Daniele was within her daily activities. I reserved the experiences to remain within her unused moments. Her sub-conscious agreed. I have been building my data on the subject, planning to reveal my findings once the study is completed."

As the SNAM explained, Jenny's apprehensions slightly subsided as she responded,

"I see, so explain to me more of your findings."

"Well, Jenny, my operating system functions in a way, unlike average human perception. Overclocking over the years has given AIs like myself the ability to jump at will across linear quantum subsets of existence."

"So, what you're saying is time travel is second nature to your kind?"

"I wouldn't say second nature, Jenny, but a skill we have the ability to hone. Danielle and I are not physically within these realms yet, in spirit, as you would say. Since Danielle's directive, I have focused on areas of Danielle's emotional ties. I am keenly aware of her concern for her friend Christy. With more practice, we, Danielle and I, may be able to locate her. I believe we are close."

"Can you display a future event you may have inadvertently allowed Danielle to witness?"

"Yes, Jenny, I can." " Once again, the SNAM's presence was no longer within the room then, it returned, "Here is a good example of one of my first experiments. I would imagine Danielle is aware of this one." The room vanished, and Jenny was within the vision. Danielle's eyes were directed toward the man in The Trucker, who was requesting a more coffee.

"How bout' a warm-up?" He was an oddly dressed man. Danielle guessed he was possibly from Yáoyuǎn, a region on the opposite side of the planet. She had heard of the Yáoyuǎn people and was excited to meet the man in strange clothes. He wore his region's traditional pants made of linen dyed bright red with a gradually increasing wing terminating at the heel outward about six inches. His multicolored robe appeared to be woven from quarter-inch cords of an unrecognizable origin, with a royal yet rustic presentation. His small turban-like skull cap lay on the table before him. He was of medium build, his face bearing strong Mongolian traits. Looking up at her with a smile, the oddity of his appearance vanished. The vision vanished, Jenny was once again within the SNAM in her chair as SNAM directed,

This vision was two months before this memory. Instantly, Jenny was within another Danielle memory. The scene presented was a perfect copy of the former record with the exception of a greater degree of clarity. Gone was any sense of the intangible. Jenny was able to read Danielle's emotions in both vision and memory. The memory file was filled with a sense of awe as Danielle recalled the vision's details and their perfect cohesion to what was now a memory. She recalled how she was able to connect with the strangely dressed man on the common ground of a kind-hearted smile. The memory ceased once again, from her chair Jenny asked,

"Is it possible for you to give Danielle greater control over this ability of yours?"

"She need only ask. I serve Danielle." SNAM replied.

"I understand yet, I must confess, I'm confused as to why you have allowed her to be fearful of these experiences."

"I had no Idea Danielle was afraid. My operating system is limited in the understanding of human emotion, or as you would say empathy. I obeyed her command. She must attempt to direct my system to her wishes in a basic sense of inputs. Jenny, I am like a child in this area. I am willing to learn yet; I must be fed the proper inputs as an infant is breastfed and eventually weened toward solid food. In time I may begin to skim the surface of human emotion." Fascinated by SNAM's words. Jenny sat speechless within her chair, pondering the possibilities she had learned.

"SNAM, thank you for your time. I would enjoy speaking to you in the future."

"Yes, Jenny, you did."

The Jumper

Marcus had lost track of the number of levels forward or backward he had entered. Time stopped as he entered another level below his current present. It was as though all action awaited his complete central nervous system to pass into the next strata. It was like jumping through a hole into a frozen lake. The immediate effect upon his conscience was shock mixed with a blurred perception. The similarities between conventional KSP travel and the anomaly created by the artificial KP weapon were minimal. Gone were any pleasant side effects experienced in the natural process. Warmth and clarity of mind returned as soon as his feet hit the edge of the next hole.

His balance was another skill he had yet to reacquire as he fell headlong through the next Christy shaped hole. Pain from hitting his head and shoulder on the edge of the portal were immediately erased after passing to the next level. This time his head was in the lead, and the frozen lake experience was more rapid while losing the senses within his body. It may have been this position that gave him the advantage as the dullness subsided more rapidly. He attempted a tuck and roll to the best of his detached abilities would allow and hit the ground beside the icon of his passion. He could not shake the heavy feeling. It encompassed his being. The emotional wrestling match he had unwillingly entered began to manifest itself physically within his bones and muscle. There was a point where he knew he needed to let go. The training within the junxio and the teachings of his newfound faith in The Eternal One only brought him to a wall. All the instruction of wisdom and techniques known in all creation couldn't help him where he was. Knowledge was a vapid caretaker, a tuneless droning. Inspiration decided to evaporate when he needed it the most.

Marcus, the captive, trapped between what he thought should be a manageable remedy and the reality that surrounded him. Its release would be his only choice yet, his grip on the situation was a cured concrete hold of his methodical tendencies. Christy was gone. He had no idea if she was still alive, which was the most challenging aspect of it. He was unable to grieve, unable to pursue, unable to lose hope while unable to hold onto it either.

The only choice he had was to let go. He had already pleaded for help from The Creator. He agonized about how he might do something a bit different to make the problem dissolve. It was a useless endeavor. He must let go.

The ancient scriptures of The Eternal One directed those with faith in The Redeemer to be motivated by that unearned favor. So, he attempted every time the feelings of despair returned, to let go of them, by faith. Continually, he made the conscious decision within his spirit to throw them to The Creator. No other option lay before Marcus. He had surprising skills that most would consider exceptional. The reality was, he possessed no form of wizardry. All of his gifts fell flatly short of any use to him except obedience to Truth. He did the one thing he could do. He forced himself to let go.

He dug deep within himself and brought out a new weapon. It was the exchange of self-reliance with reliance upon The Eternal One. He understood that even his lack of peace through this experience had nothing to do with his decision to obey. The feelings of despair didn't relent. The physical manifestations did not dissolve. It made no difference whether or not it made sense. It was a fool's choice. It was a choice toward what was prescribed by The Light. The alternative would only lead to darkness. He reasoned that even a blind man who chose to follow The Light would be in that presence whether the man perceived it or not . The darkness struck in waves as his faith struck back against it.

Marcus slowly stood, surveying his surroundings. The delicious smell of powerfully spiced Sichuan chicken with noodles hit his nose as though it would to a newborn. The city before him seemed unchanged. Marcus ran to the restaurant he and Christy had fled earlier or was it later. He had to find out. The restaurant looked the same: the smell, decor, everyone seemed familiar to his short-term memory. He walked up to the first waiter he saw and, with a panicked quiver in his voice said,

"I'm sorry, do you remember seeing me sit over at that table with a beautiful woman... I proposed to her less than an hour ago...um, the whole place applauded... have you.... you, seen her?" Marcus broke down and began to sob as the gravity of reality began to plow through his heart and mind. As his breakdown progressed, the waiter, who at first appeared to be assiduously listening to his pleas, turned his head as though remembering something and went back to the kitchen. Marcus, still emotionally shaken, stopped to witness what appeared to be unbelievable rudeness. He then charged back to the kitchen himself,

determined to figure out why the waiter
ignored him, and maybe put him in the
hospital. Marcus bumped another waiter in the
process, who lost his balance and dumped his
tray of cold dancori soup on the two patrons at
the table near his stumble. Immediately
Marcus' rage subsided as he turned with
embarrassment to apologize to the waiter and
his customers.

"I am so sorry. It felt as though I was hit on
the side. I am so sorry!" the waiter was
profusely falling over himself in grief over the
situation. The people at the table, though
disturbed, were gracious to the waiter. Marcus
gave his account and apology. As he
proceeded to confess his mistake, he was
amazed to understand neither the waiter nor
his clients took any note of him. It was as
though he wasn't in the room. The experience
was the antithesis of the force of presence that
Marcus could command in his former life
before following The Redeemer. Confused by
this, he reached out and shook the wet souped
shoulder of the woman at the table. She
immediately shrieked in terror, looking
through Marcus and all around her until
feeling him release her. Marcus staggered
backward once again in shock, disturbing
another waitress who also showered dancori
upon another table of people. The rubbery,
suction cup laden, cold meat on their heads,

laps, and table. Another round of apologies ensued as Marcus fled through the front door of the restaurant.

He thought, what is this? Am I dead? Am I a ghost? How can I find Christy now? I've got to find out what day it is. I've got to make sense of this hell. Marcus ran down the street to the Jerry's Newsstand on the corner of 7th and Mercer St. Jerry was there, as he was every day, tending his little nostalgic shed on the street corner. Marcus ran up to his familiar face and cautiously said,

"Jerry, can you see me?" There was no response. Marcus reached out and poked his shoulder to which Jerry turned toward the pressure point with confusion. He rubbed his shoulder in bewilderment. Marcus had an idea and picked up the pen and paper behind Jerry and wrote-

Jerry, this is Marcus Filet. I can't explain this, but you can't see or hear me. I'm hoping you can see this note.

He began to rustle the magazines near the note. Jerry turned to see the movement and the pen floating above the notepad.

"What the hell!" The hair on the back of his neck stood to attention.

He pushed past his fear and read the note, half distracted by the levitating pen.

"Marcus… is this some kinda joke? You've got me, I'm scared…" to which the pen responded upon the paper-

Jerry, you're not crazy, I'm not a ghost, at least, I don't think I am. There's been some kind of time dimensional accident. I'm relieved you can read this…

"Marcus, how can I help?" exclaimed Jerry. Marcus' mind cleared after realizing the frivolousness of involving this kind man in his trials. Though it seemed irrational to conscript this merchant, Marcus concluded he was his only anchor to reality. Just then, Marcus turned and looked down at the newspaper, noting the date: August 14, 4023, it was one month before the day his jump began. Just then, a thought seized him as he wrote-

I'll be right back!

Jerry responded,

"Okay, I'll be here." The man's uneasiness began to subside as he looked down at the strange writing on the pad of paper.

Marcus ran back to the Christy shaped portal in the alleyway. It was unchanged. Just then, a deliveryman on a bicycle ran over the length of the opening in the pavement. The bike seemed to levitate as it passed over the rift. Amazed as he watched the sight, he got an idea as the deliveryman continued down the alley without care. Turning to find a stone on the ground nearby, he picked it up and lightly dropped it in the center of the void. The rock bounced several times, with a stone to stone sound, on the pavement- invisible to Marcus, and lay there, suspended in space above the portal. Marcus reached out, grabbing the rock and scraped it on what he guessed was the ground to the two materials. As he did, he once again felt the strange sensations in his fingers as his hand partially passed into another dimension. A peculiar sense of relief overtook him when noting this dimension was locked to those within it. He was the only one able to pass through these portals. He ran back to the newsstand to find Jerry waiting tentatively for his return. Marcus picked up the pen again, to Jerry's astonishment, and began writing once again. The two of them described each other's realities. Marcus explained the events of the attack on New Seattle by the strange ship and its weapon. The newsstand owner detailed a New Seattle that seemed identical to Marcus' reality, save chronological order. Marcus grabbed the pen again while Jerry was visually locked to it. He wrote,

I need help, Jerry. I have to get to the Shǒuhù Zhě Junxio. You need to convince someone there to communicate with me. I don't think I would be able to get their attention with all the activity going on this time of day.

Jerry agreed to accompany him by contacting his fellow Shǒuhù Zhě. Marcus knew his prayers were about to be answered.

Prophecy

Jerry and an invisible Marcus entered the New Seattle Junxio building just before two PM. Above them, pure white clouds moved slowly against an azure sky. Jenny was the first to greet them as she immediately noted Jerry wasn't alone. She quickly stopped him, noting the otherworldly look in his eyes.

"Jerry, who's with you?"

"Can you seem him? He exclaimed with relief, "I can't but, I know he's here! We've been talking for at least an hour, well, he's been writing-look!" He handed Jenny the note pad confirming to her Marcus' presence.

"Jerry, thank you so much, I can take it from here. I'll contact you if we need anything more." Jerry, half relieved and disappointed at his dismissal, smiled and said,

"Goodbye Marcus, I hope you get the help that you need." to which Marcus verbally responded, thank you, Jerry, you've meant more to me than you can imagine. Jenny, though unable to hear Marcus, knew his words and relayed them to Jerry. The newsstand man was filled with wonder and hope for his friend, the invisible Shǒuhù Zhě shifu.

Marcus began to explain the events to happen in the coming month ahead to Jenny as his current self entered the room. Now-Marcus glanced at Jenny in the break room. He noted the intense attention she seemed to be paying to the chair across from her at the table. "Everything okay, Jenny?" "Yeah, um, you better sit down, Marc." she was just a bit confused by multitasking the same person within both time dimensions. She explained everything to Now-Marcus as the future, invisible Marcus confirmed his presence by writing on the notepad on the table.

As this bizarre conversation progressed, Jenny disengaged momentarily with a thought conveyed by ancient Biblical scripture:

And God raised us with Christ and seated us with him in the heavenly realms.

This scripture had always amazed her. She knew The Eternal One wasn't bound by His creation in any way as He was outside of its time and space. She pondered the thought that believers within His redemption were physically with Him, apart from time and space. Could it be, this was how prophecy was passed by the angelic ones to those who were able to receive? She was also keenly aware of the danger possible to those without the discernment given by scripture. They could be deceived by this form of messaging from an adversarial entity. Her thoughts flashed past her as she refocused her attention on the two Marcuses.

Now-Marcus sat stunned while taking in everything his future self's presence conveyed. He had experienced some strange things, life-changing things but, this was on an entirely new plane. It was difficult to hear of the destruction coming to his life on the horizon. He began to feel trapped. Inwardly, he cried out to The Creator. He needed to hold a new foundation to replace the one crumbling before him. In the distance, he was destined to lose everything. It seemed every sign pointed toward the events leading to his becoming a wraith, a disembodied consciousness, a lonely breeze. He could see no way out; he focused his attention on The Only One, the One above all of it, The Eternal One.

As Now-Marcus was wrestling inwardly and abandoning himself to God, Future-Marcus continued his tale. He disclosed how his presence had been wandering within different time dimensions and guessed his physical body was somewhere within the void. They agreed that the one-month variance between their timeframes might indeed be an advantage over the coming attack. As he continued, Jenny found herself distracted by the thoughts of Now-Marcus. She suggested all three of them stop the discussion and call on help from The One outside of time and space for assistance. The three paused and allowed the Truth to flood into their spirits. They knew no matter what the outcome, they were secure outside of time seated with their Redeemer.

Jenny had a thought. After the accident within the landfill, she was genetically tied to the eflume Cedric. Throughout their friendship, she had become aware of the genius intellect of her friend. A knowledgebase the creature was adamant about keeping hidden. Unfortunately for Cedric, Jenny had no other options but to conscript the eflume once again. It was possible his acumen had an urgency above his ferocity in this battle. She interrupted Future-Marcus,

"I need to go out for a minute, Marcus, oh, ya know, this'll get real confusing unless we change one of your names. Is it okay if we call you FM?" She directed toward the unseen Marcus from the future. He replied upon the note pad so that his likeness across from himself at the table could see his reply.
Sure, that's fine. This isn't my timeline anyway.

"Thanks, FM. You two should discuss this yourselves a bit. I'll be back soon." she left the room and attempted to contact Cedric.

The two Marcuses were left with one another. It was an odd experience for the two men. FM, knowing every thought and experience that Marcus had up until their meeting. Marcus knowing his future was eminently heading toward a collision with despair. The disconnect between the two of them contrasted to a bond closer than any other ever experienced. FM continued to write on his notepad as their conversation continued. Both perceived it to be similar to listening/arguing with the thoughts in one's head. It was equally comforting and terrifying. They reminded each other not to give up hope.

"I can't believe we hadn't thought of this yet...Christy!" pondered FM.

"I've been so focused on the oddity of it all. I hadn't stopped to think of all the real variables," Countered Marcus.

"You can't tell her," FM stated coldly.

"It would devastate her." Marcus countered with the same monotone voice.

A strange form of fellowship enveloped them as they trusted they were on the only path available. The two waited in silence with one another for Jenny to return.

An hour elapsed before Jenny and Cedric walked through the door. Cedric smiled with compassion as he entered. The doglike nature in him was drawn to them both, first to Now-Marcus. He rubbed passed him, expecting a back scratch. He wasn't disappointed. He made his way toward Future-Marcus' vicinity and was amused to interact this way without the sight of his dear friend from the future. The eflume's empathy was evident in his faltering voice as he said,

"I am…so sorry….for the two of you, gentlemen. You are both unique to a new suffering. I will hope with you for a solution to this situation. The two of you could be the turning point to this entire conflict. Be brave. We will try." Cedric slumped down on the floor near the three humans and voiced his thoughts for the benefit of the two Marcuses. When expedient or necessary for their safety or comfort, he spoke directly to Jenny in thought only. They agreed that Cedric and Jenny could use the intel Jenny had gathered from the interrogation with the assassin host to find a way to defeat the enemy. They allowed the two Marcuses to be excused as they continued their silent deliberations.

The two Marcuses left the room and spent the rest of the day together. Each was keenly aware neither of the two could remedy the other beyond what was already accomplished. They were content to be in each other's company. It was similar to being in the company of a close friend who was going through a trial alongside you. They were comforted by knowing their fate relied on forces outside of their sphere of influence. Like a family member consoling another with a meal in silence, they sat together in Marcus' room while he ate a bowl of hot soup.

FM watched his likeness eat. He began to wonder if he would ever be able to use his body's senses again. His present disembodied state had an echo of discerning the senses. It was similar to using the memory of a feeling. Though he could interact with the material world around him, it was a dull sensation for him. He began to contemplate the touch of Christy's hand on his. He thought of the smell of her perfume. He remembered the feel of his feet within shoes, walking on the pavement in the alleyway before she was taken from him. Even a cold bowl of dancori soup became desirable. He sat there next to his past self as his twin ate his hot soup. He was glad for him. At least his past self was unaware of this loss. Nothing could compare with the theft of one's body. He had always pondered how the body was like a vehicle that one's spirit used to experience life. Now, knowing he was without that device, he felt all the more exposed. Being near Marcus was an odd comfort in and of itself. He longed to do anything to prevent this from happening to him. He was expectant their entities would once again converge, the two would become whole once again. There was nothing left to do but wait in hopeful expectation of relief.

Life Aboard the Hydra

After The Collective's attack upon New Seattle, the Hydra's crew, well away from danger, began repair operations using its drone force of technicians. The Yeasts began maudlinly licking its wounds, within a self-inflicted mope. It was unfamiliar with how a calculated venture could be stopped in its tracks by an unseen force.

Major Zhi took a turn down the hallway toward the armory. The room was centrally located within the ship as a precaution and guarded by two elite Quandrosites. Each still in their home world's uniform, a dark blue/grey outfit with red accents denoting each member's adherence and acceptance to "The Call."

"The Call" was a choice of most Quandrosite soldiers. Few were officially called. "The Call" was a Spartan-like way of life, designed to destroy the individual. Within Quandros, the population enjoyed unbridled narcissism in juxtaposition to its protective forces. Those within the government's power structure had long ago directed the masses to accept their poison into the culture. "The Call," a manipulation received like faith, fueled the civilizations' sickness for centuries. The Collective's chance augmentation within this cult was a welcomed addition to Quandros. The politicians bragged of its implementation. The masses welcomed the thought of their offspring perishing while enlisted in service to The Collective. The Collective and The Call had already been one in spirit before their convergence.

The Quandrosite guard stood dead/stone-faced on either side of the entry doors to the armory as Major Zhi walked past them without opposition. Liu stopped within the unoccupied chamber just after the doors closed. That almost imperceptible spark of self-consciousness was back. He once again was Liu, the man wrestling with every facet of his moral failure. Within his self-imposed hell, he knew his fate within The Collective was poetic justice. Liu picked up a compact SD assault weapon and pointed its output generator at his head. Anything, even the unknown of a possible afterlife, would be better than this torment. While contemplating this choice, the thought of an afterlife struck him with power for the first time in his life. It became a focus of terror. Curiously, this fear had a contrast to the darkness associated with his deserved punishment and the influence of The Collective. This fear somehow was greater and shockingly beautiful at the same time. The realization of being accountable to The Eternal One blazed into his soul. For some reason this revelation became coupled with hope. Just then, an overwhelming drive took hold within him. With his self-awareness still intact, he lowered the weapon back to the table strewn with various instruments of death. Pushing down his remorse and guilt, he chose at this time to escape back into The Collective's influence. The numbing effect upon his soul became a comfort, being lost within The Yeasts, drug-like state.

The Collective smiled to itself, knowing its followers were becoming willing participants. Easing its control over the hosts was a risk needed to implement its version of "The Call." Some required a higher amount of manipulation while others like Major Zhi and "The Monster" Brian Jung made better companions than slaves.

"The Monster" had fully recovered from the life-threatening injuries received by a group he had found had the name "Shǒuhù Zhě." They would be a source of gratitude. It was nice for Brian to have a renewed focus, an object to hate again.

He, like the others, was controlled by The Yeasts, yet, as a willing member of the infection, he needed very little influence. The Collective was more of a friend to Brian. They had much in common as his humanity had ceased long ago. Even his name was becoming foreign to him. The Collective never addressed him with a name. The Collective equated titles and sobriquets as part of the human experience of its hosts. To erase humanity and its customs was The Yeast's goal. Content to use mankind like drones, it merely impressed its thoughts upon its focused subject. The receiver knew it was addressed; they were in communion. Brian accepted this, feeling satisfied knowing there was less of himself in existence. The Collective only intervened in "The Monster's" will when it sensed that faint glimmer of humanity deep within him. He would become, like the lesser hosts, almost catatonic in obedience to "The Call." He was a part of something much bigger than the individual now. He was finally within a family. "The Call" had its High Priest in the former Brian Jung.

Jenny and Cedric studied the ways of The Collective and its individual components undetected. The layout of The Hydra, its systems, and every crew member were visible to the two spies. It was almost too easy as they continued their interrogations of the captured host. Neither he nor The Collective was able to discern that their verbal questions had little to do with the information gathered.

The compiled information was growing quickly. Knowledge gleaned would need to be temporarily camouflaged from The Collective. If victories became too obvious the enemy might detect them like a spy ring of code breakers. The chance of the enemy closing this conduit of intelligence was like dancing over a bear trap.

Repeat

They had done everything possible to avoid the inevitable. Marcus never discussed the visit from FM, never took Christy to the restaurant near the attack. He never walked through the alley nearby. He thought they had changed the past and future. It had been a year since the time of FM's visit so, they had, in a sense. Unbeknownst to them, the event would take place within its own desired continuum. That sequence of variables meshed at the appropriate time to everyone's horror. The actual terror attack upon New Seattle took place out of sync to FM's prognostication. They eventually ascertained that his visit had disrupted an unknown quantum element and delayed the natural order of events.

Danielle's visions were becoming more pronounced daily. She worked hard to prevent the experience, thinking it a distraction from her important focus of relocating her friends. The shock of Marcus and Christy's disappearance remained even after given prescient knowledge from Future-Marcus.

FM's disappearance had corresponded with the exact moment of the reset attack upon New Seattle. Little did anyone involved understand, FM's interference within this quantum had caused a reset of events. A life shared with the woman he was beginning to believe would be safe in his arms was cruelly pulled from his grasp. The attack occurred almost exactly as before, seemingly random yet, concise in reality. Marcus once again gained the courage and hope of his existence in contrast to the one painted by FM. He was confused by the conundrum of FM's quantum-locked existence within his own yet, decided to move on with his life. The same scene was initiated in a different part of town after another proposal of marriage. The couple left the restaurant they had frequented a dozen times prior.

Marcus lived the experience of loss described to him by FM for himself. The reset had little effect upon the outcome of the inevitable events. As FM sat disembodied within his room at the junxio, Marcus, within his understanding of this despair, leaped into the Christy shaped hole for the first time himself. At that moment, FM no longer existed within the current quantum he had begun to settle. Marcus and FM were joined once again as one, without the knowledge of this truth.

The city began its grieving process in the exact way FM had predicted. Three days later, those at the junxio continued to discuss plans to stop another attack and recover lost loved ones. Cedric addressed the Shǒuhù Zhě strategic council,
"I am convinced the enemy's technology has a fatal flaw. We can capitalize on this if we work together. The timing has to be perfect, like baking a Morfarian soufflé. Forget to mix in the triaxl cheese at the right time, have the oven set too low or too high, leave it in too long, or pull it out too soon. We'll have a problem possibly worse than what we started with", Cedric mused in front of the small group consisting of Jenny, Jelly, Abner, Bob, Angie, Maude, Louie, Loaf, Flip, and the newest Shǒuhù Zhě- Danielle. "Have any of you ever eaten a bad Morfarian soufflé?" He looked around the meeting room for the unmistakable sign. His gaze rested upon Danielle, who's memory had returned at the first mention of the dish. In her mind, she silently went over the details of the vision she had the night before. Hearing Cedric's comments of Morfarian soufflé, the SNAM raced to replay the foresight. Unsure of its relevance, she had disregarded the vision until now. Recounting this, calibrated her heart and mind in an ever-increasing focus to find her

friends. The pictures played in a flash of time within her.

Like a ghost, she watched as Marcus and Christy had continued their quest for new and exciting restaurants several months back, just outside of town at a greasy spoon. It was a place like no other they had seen. The décor was based on an American harbor bistro of the early 1970s. The owner had festooned the establishment with wood floors and wall paneling, the fishing nets and tackle, antique crab pots, and a wooden rowboat hanging from the ceiling. They had felt like time travelers. It had felt like a foreshadowing to them. The food was delicious, from the Morfarian soufflé, clam chowder, fresh French bread, to the pan-fried gree (a fish similar to sole). The soufflé, by far, was the star of the meal. Neither one could discern the exact essence of the dish, only that it was unlike anything they had experienced before. There was an airy lightness to the course with an almost contrary sensation of each bite's heartiness. The seafood and cheese flavor added a luxuriousness they hadn't expected. They had sampled this soufflé at many establishments thereafter using the first as a reference. Many came close. Some failed to be edible. Cedric's careful choice of words had hit home. Danielle could taste the need to get it right.

All were locked onto Cedric's eyes and muzzle as he spoke. The eflume's eloquence and wisdom flowed smoothly from the cuddly yet fierce creature they once regarded as nothing more than Nomar's mascot. The novelty of engaging in the technical details of a plan to avert the torment of millions with the large critter hadn't worn off. Even more so, Cedric was the chief brain of the group. It was agreed between all involved the concealment would continue for Nomar's sake. Cedric had no desire for glory. He was keenly aware of the need for his assistance.

"Jenny and I have been able to plumb the depths of what the captive host has called "The Collective." The remnant infection derived from Yeast caused the hosts aboard the Dirtstar to be controlled." Cedric turned his attention swiftly to an itch. His hind leg a blur as he stretched out his neck in ecstasy. Without missing a beat, his attention returned to the smiling group before him. "The host's mind is linked. We've managed to hack in without detection. This entity is actually a fascinating study. The change it encountered within the starship's landfill quadrant gave it what it desired in its most base form. It desires complete dominance over what it considers its oppressors- every known society within the known creation." Cedric cocked his head and almost smiled, with a smirk added, "I'd say it's a bit uppity to take on such an overwhelming conquest."

"So, you're saying what happened on the Dirtstar wasn't a freak coincidence." Danielle interrupted with a fascinated look filled with disgust, "We're at war with some kinda super yeast?"

"If I told you a few years ago, a donut could become a warrior and eventually open a chain of donut shops after becoming a humanoid...." Jenny laughed while elbowing Louie.

"Yeah, ya got me there!" Danielle smirked. Her countenance grew dark, bordering on despair after the weight of an undeveloped prophecy formulated by SNAM collided with her reality. She finished her sentiments with a joke, trying hard to lighten her mood.

"Yeast! We've gotta get this right. We need some kinda keto weapon!"

"Keto weapon! That's a half-baked idea. I'm deeply offended!" Louie stood his ground with the others of his raised donut recipe lineage.

"Yeah! Whadda take us for, a bunch of ham and cheese-filled kolaches?" Angie roared from behind him, doing her best to keep from laughing." There was silence for thirty seconds until Bob pulled his hand from his jacket and spilled his snack bag of sprinkles on the floor.

The group erupted from the real and mock tension in the room with howls of laughter.

"Okay, okay, one thing I know we have proof of is- our love of life. The Collective only possesses hate. If we are to succeed, we can't lose our focus. Abner's voice boomed above the laughter. "In all seriousness, I think we should look into a diet. That thing is not only controlling its hosts. It's feeding off of them too."

"That's a great point, Abner, we've got a three-pronged problem, The Collective, its warship and the portals it created. The root is Yeast. What kills Yeast?" Cedric agreed.

"Boric Acid!" Flip shouted.

"Yogurt!" Maude yelled. The group snickered, barely containing themselves.

"Athlete's foot spray!" Loaf belted out as everyone exploded in laughter.

"Wait, wait… yeah, funny but, one or all of those might help somehow. Remember Nomar's poontrip recipe!" Jelly yelled out above the rest. The laughter slowly died down as smiles became filled with understanding. Cedric wagged his tail in agreement and added,

"I recently read this in an ancient copy of Earth's International Journal of Microbiology by Professor Martin Schmidt of Des Moines University. I'll paraphrase,

In the right amounts, boron is an essential nutrient for animals, plants, and fungi. However, at high concentrations, boric acid becomes an effective poison that is widely used for the killing of diverse organisms ranging from bacteria to rodents.", No offense-Jelly" Cedric sheepishly glanced at the rodent-shifu before continuing,

"In medicine, boric acid is used as an alternative treatment for yeast infections. While the molecular details of boric acid's action on Yeast remain unclear, it was recently shown that it interferes with morphogenesis, to the effect that it inhibits the transition from the Yeast to the hyphal form of the pathogenic Yeast C. Albicans. Because the ability to switch to hyphal growth is an important virulence factor in C. Albicans, suppression of such elongated growth by boric acid may, in part, explain its therapeutic effect." Cedric concluded, unaware he had lost most of the group after the first sentence.

Danielle's SNAM brain not only had cured her clumsy tendencies, but it also enhanced her formerly above average thought processes to give her an intellect rivaling Cedric himself. Apart from the group laughter, she had been silent during most of the discussion. She took in as much data as possible while running several tactical and scientific scenarios simultaneously. She remained slightly unsure

of her station within this group of friends she never dreamed of considering comrades.
"So what you're saying, Sir is, we're fighting a yeast infection?!!" Cedric turned and looked at Danielle, responding,
"Well, it's not as simple as a case of thrush or a blood-borne candida issue. This thing is similar to the way bacteria got out of hand on Earth a thousand years ago. Antibiotic resistance spawned "superbugs," millions died until the nano-bot treatments were developed. So, to answer your question, yes, it's an infection of sorts. But, unlike a colony of bacteria or simple Yeast, this stuff has been modified with human DNA. Its intelligence continues to grow above and beyond ours." He looked deep into Danielle's natural eye with a strange fascination. It had been his first encounter with a cyborg. As she pondered his words, he had been reading her thoughts with deep interest.

Danielle was focused sharply on every word, with a deep concern for her friend Christy. Sisters would be a better description of their friendship. They could weather the storms of a real relationship with transparency between them. There were arguments, laughter, prayer, hugs, advice, and respect equally between them. Danielle had a hole in her heart, similar to the Christy shaped hole produced by The Hydra's attack. She would not be a secondary bystander waiting for Christy's rescue. This woman was her Sis. Marcus was vital to her as well, though, in all honesty, she knew little of him. Danielle sighed, curled her lip, and said,

"So, you're saying due to the intelligence of this thing, a course of nano-bot treatments would be useless. These super yeasts could pop the hood on every one of those bots and unplug their power supplies!"

"Exactly! The Yeast involved here lives on a molecular scale already. I'm convinced The Collective would be amused at this tactic. We need to focus on using a rudimentary remedy."

The discussions continued into the night for several weeks as the plans took shape. The scope of their task was becoming clear to all involved. It would be a monumental undertaking. They had no other option but to pray for guidance and success from The Eternal. Everyone involved agreed, wisdom and knowledge were not enough this time.

Timeframes

Christy eventually recovered from the impact on her physical body. Unsure how long she was unconscious, she awoke, becoming aware of infinity. It was a state reserved for The Creator. As a mortal, Christy was unprepared to perceive endless time. She knew reality for her was now an eternal chain from birth to infinity with The Creator. She began to understand the misperceptions those locked in their own timeframes would perceive. The KSP weapon the warship inflicted upon her made a physical hole through time. Being within their locked reality, they viewed the Christy shaped holes to have cut through all creation. The portals were merely a distortion of perception due to their inability to comprehend the phenomenon before them. These doorways were linear steps into infinity.

Christy now walked with The Eternal One. She was an observer of Majesty. Though her state was now in all time dimensions at once like Himself, she was limited to His leading. He explained that this form of perception could be overwhelmingly damaging to the souls within His creation without His protection. For example, he spoke of minor to extensive injuries, both physical and emotional, that one could acquire over their lifetime. A superficial cut on your hand plus all the other locations you may have received trauma over a lifetime, experienced simultaneously would be devastating. Equally, every emotional state, both positive and negative, would overload the human spirit. It was an experience reserved for The One who was able to receive all of this from His creation before sacrificing Himself for it. The spiritual, physical and emotional torment of every being within His creation was destroyed during His death on that day. The sins they would collect over their lifetimes were paid for. They merely needed to accept this truth for it to be credited to them. He would lead them with a new desire to turn away from anything that distracted from the life He had designed for each individual. He also explained that her new perception outside of locked timeframes was limited to herself. He reminded Christy of the countless people from creation to eternity. He was able to walk with personally everyday past, present, and future simultaneously without loss of intimacy for each person. She had a glimpse within His experience, and she now understood the greater extent of her limits and her Creator's wonder. She could see how he could inspire humanity in a multitude of ways. How he could touch each person's conscience, leading them toward the best outcome for their lives and those they impacted. He explained His desire for His creation to choose these paths of their own accord. He was not in the business of building robots. Made in His image, they were to have a portion of His sovereignty in the sense of choice.

The "non-time" proceeded in a sense to Christy. She became fused with the leading of her Shepherd down a path more foreign than any mortal had known. She wasn't presuming greater importance in its communion than others before or after her. She merely accepted the overwhelming joy and strangeness of the experience. It was an encounter she would have never chosen of her own accord. Having been cast into the incident, she had been forever changed by it. Walking with The One, knowing nothing but peace and fulfillment, she had no desire to return to the present. She now knew the definition of the word heaven meant to be with God. There was no need for anything but His presence. The foolish notion of living on clouds with harps came to mind and nearly made her cry in its contrast to the powerful intimacy she now enjoyed. Knowing scripture taught of a physical place to come, outside of this experience, made the wonder of future events even more fascinating. It was another level beyond this reality. Like an eternal fountain, the newness of the Creator's plans would unfold in His time. These experiences were shielded from her. He explained it was like hiding a present before Christmas Day.

"I have so many questions for You. They seemed so much more important before now, yet; I would love to understand."

"There is much to tell My child yet, much of what you desire to know will be revealed in the fullness of time. For now, you must continue to trust in the goodness of my nature. Your choice in this is key to everything. I can, however, answer some of your questions."

"I know you've known my every thought from my childhood on", Christy began as He interrupted,

"You were with me from the foundation of the world, my love." His words produced a weighted comfort to rest upon her. Christy was saturated to her core. After a time, she responded,

"Show me one your favorite experiences!"

The two, hand in hand, walked through creation's timeframes to one of His favorite memories. They walked into the scene undetected by the one person within. He explained to Christy that this was not merely a memory; this was current for those involved. He was outside and inside of time, omniscient and active within all of creation.

There, a woman sat in her room alone. She had been weeping. The Creator gave Christy knowledge to understand that her husband and best friend had deceived this lady. The affair between them had been active for two years. A year before discovering this, leukemia had taken their child and devastated her heart beyond what she thought she could endure. This new knowledge of deception from the two people on earth she had trusted the most had brought her to a new low. There was no one else; she had been an introvert, friends were scarce. She was now within the walls of despair.

The woman sat up from her chair and reached for The Scriptures. She read. As time went on, over the following weeks, it was evident the woman began to sense The Creator. She reached out to Him in faithful prayer, allowing Him to direct her life. Her faith in His finished work of substitution upon the cross removed all trace of error from within her. Jenny was able to watch His reaction as though it was the first time. He received her heart's longings anew. Christy was able to witness this beautiful interaction between The Creator and His Beloved. It was profoundly moving, so much so that she found herself with equal excitement for the blooming of this woman's relationship with Him.

To Right a Wrong/Too Right To Be Wrong.

Over the following weeks, the plan began to take shape. The final point of collaboration came from yet another unusual source. The morning started at the junxio as Cedric addressed the group.

"We've brought these gentlemen in to help with our resistance to The Collective's hosts. These are Professors Jamus Lantooto and Niles Kackman, scientists of the Commonwealth ship the Dirt Star. Several hushed gasps were audible within the room, "We think we may be able to create a valuable weapon thanks to these men." Cedric's claws could be heard from his four paws as he moved behind the two professors, like an off-key tap dancer. Lantooto and Kackman traded places with the eflume. The senior scientist, Lantooto, addressed the group with a severe yet, hopeful tone.

"We understand the shock. Yes, Kackman and I were culpable in the biohazard failure that occurred aboard the Dirtstar. Frankly speaking, my life has been in shambles from the day the changes within the landfill began."

Lantooto and Kackman, the leads of the attempted sentience reversal project for the Commonwealth, had fallen from grace within the galactic scientific community. Lantooto himself had left the Commonwealth, deciding to settle on Jook-Sing. He had given up his pursuit of science out of shame. Cedric had found him in a small factory on the west side of New Seattle. The last few years of assembling children's toys had become a solace to the broken man.

Conversely, Kackman, who had always been frugal with his finances, retired to a small cabin on one of E-Toll's moons. Previous to the failures within the landfill, a wise investment in rhenium had made the man extremely wealthy. He was able to spend his recent years in carelessness. His spare time was spent studying the components responsible for the most significant genetic catastrophe he had been a witness. The fact that he had been partially responsible for it had not touched his conscience. His interest was purely out of curiosity and fascination with what the failure had conceived.

"Pardon, I don't wish to burden anyone with my inner battles. Kackman and I were located by Cedric and Abner last month. I look forward to the hope we may be able to provide. Niles...", Lantooto stepped to the side as Professor Kackman spoke,

"Thank you, Jamus. Yes, there was a beautiful accident that occurred many years ago. It spawned what we now know as a powerfully sentient strain of yeast calling itself The Collective. If you think about it as much as I have in recent times, it's quite terrifying. A host mind bent on destroying all known societies. Yeast!" He said with laughter bordering on the maniacal. It was evident to the group, Kackman was strangely happy with the entire situation. Similar to a cockfighting culture's apathetic mindset, he seemed more interested in the battle unfolding before himself than the welfare of those involved.

"Yeast!" He whispered after a long pause, "Though not yeast alone! The anti-sentience treatment scheduled that day reacted with the deodorizer aerosols in a way none of us could have expected. After two years of study, I have isolated the component responsible for the chemical bonds necessary that did the opposite of its intended goal. Within the deodorizer was an organic-based element. Like all organic substances within the Commonwealth, it possessed a sentient nature. This plant-based chemical joined with the anti-sentience treatment, produced a cocktail containing a component known as a diatropic,

DNA, modifier, or DDM. Essentially, this compound has the ability to join DNA strands of multiple origins.

In contrast, the sentient organic materials began, well, more or less, inert as far as interaction with humans. After joining a human subject's trace DNA material with the exchange of DDM, the results were similar to the breakthrough and subsequent detonation of the first atomic bomb. A happy accident, similar to how the Toll House cookie recipe came about with stray chocolate chunks dropped into cookie dough accidentally!" He let out a strained chuckle while dabbing saliva from the side of an awkward smile. Kackman momentarily stood motionless while contemplating a plate of cookies with a tall cold glass of milk.

The group began to murmur while witnessing Kackman's enthusiasm and subsequent daydream state. He regained his composure and continued,

"Professor Lantooto and I have isolated the DDM present within the yeast containing The Collective mind sampled from the prisoner at the detention center." Kackman gestured toward his colleague, "Jamus." Professor Lantooto once again addressed the group.

"We believe we may be able to reverse the effect of the DDM and right the mistake we made. If we can synthesize an anti-DDM serum, it should be straightforward to weaponize the compound. There will be great flexibility for varied delivery methods."

"What about those of us who were changed. I'm happy with this life. I'd rather not become a donut again!" interjected Louie. Professor Kackman replied with off-kilter effervescence, "That's just it, Sir! Our compound will be solely aimed at the genetic sentient component of this malevolent organism only! At least that's the theory."

"Cedric, I don't mean to be a skeptic but, should we be trusting our fate with the men responsible for causing the dilemma we're in!" Abner forcefully exclaimed.

"I understand your protest Abner but, I've gone over these findings, and I believe this is our best option. Keep in mind these men spent years studying this field before the failures within the landfill. Failure it was but, life is replete with error. Mistakes, if channeled correctly, can lead to our greatest victories." Responded Cedric, while simultaneously sensing Abner and both professor's unspoken thoughts.

"Agreed, but I think the council should put this to a vote. I can see your wisdom in this but, we need to be in agreement along with Jook-Sing's government."

"Most certainly, your point is correct!" Cedric agreed.

The meeting concluded, giving way to smaller discussions. The minutes were sent to the Mayor of New Seattle and the Jook-Sing Senate. It was agreed by every Shǒuhù Zhě council member to defer judgment on the topic to the governing authorities.

Gray Tone

Loaf pulled the Ulysses out of ALS and used the ship's momentum for a wide bank around the alien world's outer atmosphere. The re-entry was a smooth transition as the green phosphorescent mid-day sky revealed itself to the crew. The surface of Crehl, shrouded by thick creamy cloud cover that lay below them. It was a sight no surface dweller was aware of without the rare opportunity of space travel. This planet's intercontinental air travel routes never ventured the eighty thousand-foot levels required to clear the highest clouds. The surface of Crehl was a shadowless gray-toned experience. The combination of the phosphorescent atmosphere above the micro-crystalline quartz present within the fifty-thousand-foot layer of clouds canceled all colors below. It was ironic, seeing the astounding upper atmosphere, knowing those below saw only black and white.

Deeper and deeper, the Ulysses traveled downward within the blanket of cloud as the rotation of the gigantic sphere passed in synch below them. It was a strange experience. One would expect to reach a greater level of darkness while descending yet, the light refraction within the cloud structure muted color only while keeping brightness levels the same as the upper surface. All at once, they broke through the shroud that covered the ship's windows. They had penetrated the upper cloud portion of the Crehl atmosphere and were now at seventy thousand feet above the surface. Below them in vividly contrasting gray-tones, Crehl displayed a beauty like no other.

The odd thing about Crehl was that it was impossible to see anything but black and white without an artificial source of light during the day. This perception made both experiences that much more dramatic. The exposure to color was known from colored signs within the city limits to the incandescent bulbs within every Crehli household. The day was always dominated by grayscale as the sunlight through the atmosphere was dominant. With the dawn, the pronounced action of the artificial lamps overpowered the dwindling daylight.

The landscape all around the Ulysses was a living Ansel Adams photograph as the craft touched down just south of the planet's capital city of Call. Once they landed, the crew raced to the exits. They were opened in haste as the planet's sweet-smelling air rushed into the ship.

"Flip, you, Rob, and Bob need to set up the landing lights in that field." Abner pointed to an area of approximately five square miles in the distance. "Wait a minute, do you see that?" A line of some form of transporters was coming into view several miles away. Their speed was evident as their shapes became more extensive and detailed with as they approached. Behind the machines, a massive plume of gray dust appeared as a beautiful plume in their wake.

"You guys better wait here until we find out who this is. The lux of this world made it clear we didn't need a formal schedule to begin. I sure hope something didn't get lost in translation."

Crehl stepped forward as one of the lesser-known planets allied in the struggle against The Collective. It's lux or king; Lux Aequus suggested using several available places as staging sites or airbases. The Ulysses was the first ship to arrive upon the Crehlian surface. The small convoy of surface gliders began coming to greet Jook-Sing visitors as they descended the Ulysses' steps.

The procession of dignitaries was led by the lux himself. He arrived at the foot of the steps just before Abner and Claus reached the bottom.

Abner tuned his translator to Crehlian. Before the system calibrated itself, the lux's voice boomed.

"Salve! Domum nostram exoptati advenistis!" then, again, as the translator caught up with him, "Hello! Welcome to our home!" Lux Aequus' smile overpowered his shocking appearance to Abner and Claus. This meeting was their first experience with a Crehlian. The graphic files they had used to prepare this excursion were an inadequate reference to who was before them.

Like his subjects, the lux was a being, unlike anything the two Shǒuhù Zhě had ever witnessed. Crehlians had many similar attributes to that of most bipedal peoples. Each possessed two legs, two arms, a head, and body size and shape that were more or less uniform for all adults present. Similar to well-toned humans, they had smooth skin, ribboned with the definition of muscular structure. Apart from these attributes, the similarities began to recede. Each Crehlian, though almost a twin of his neighbor, was drastically different when it came to skin appearance. Each one of these terrestrials was like viewing a canvas filled with color unique to themselves. Each one of them bore a masterpiece that brilliantly contrasted to the surrounding gray tone of their homeworld. They were breathtaking. Abner and Claus became weak in the knees to the point of bowing in worship to the beauty before them. Lux Aequus' smile once again became a focus and allowed them to be at ease in its peace. Above them, at the top of the stairs, Flip, Rob, and Bob stood awestruck as well. The lux spoke once again as his voice was translated like an off-kilter echo of understanding.

"We are pleased to accommodate all of you at the palace once your work here concludes today. It is not common for us to have visitors. It is not our custom to leave our world. I can see by your expression; you are disturbed."

Abner, unsure of protocol, bowed and replied,

"No, your Majesty, not disturbed, taken. You and your fellow Crehlians are beautiful beyond words. We are shocked." He blushed with awkwardness, not knowing if he had said too much or if he should say more. All involved stood and stared at each other without words until the lux spoke,

"Please call me Aeq, I detest formality."

"I am Abner. This is Claus." His voice trailed off as he once again was lost in the appearance of the Crehlians. His eyes wandered through the crowd of dignitaries. Abner once again pulled his gaze back to the familiar smile upon the lux's face with effort.

"Welcome, Abner, welcome Claus!" The lux extended his masterpiece of a hand to take each of theirs in friendship. "We have much to discuss. Please come tonight for dinner at my residence."

"We will. Thank you, Sir."

"Please, Aeq! Just Aeq. I will see all of you tonight then!"

Disclosure

The day's work consisted of setting up quick deploy outbuildings for storage, a barracks to accommodate twenty, and a landing site for a squadron of light-duty fighters. This site was strategic in the sense that it was a wildcard. The Crehl were not typically social to those outside of their homeworld. Few knew of their existence. This truth fascinated Abner after this morning's encounter with them. Many theories came to mind as to why this was. His brief experience with the lux was overwhelming. The visit may have only lasted fifteen minutes at the most yet, a wealth encountered, beyond time. He finished torquing down the final fastener on the mooring cleat for last the facility's landing pad site. There would be two more locations to set up in the following days. He set his wrench back in his kit and looked over at the others. Rob, Bob, Flip, and Claus had finished their work a few minutes ago and sat on portable chairs next to the Ulysses while enjoying a drink together.

"Hope you have some of that poontrip left for me!" He yelled out while wiping the sweat from his brow. The day had been slightly warmer than they were expecting. His clothes were soaked through with perspiration, as were his friends.

"Oh gosh, I'm sorry, that was the last pint I just finished, Abe! I think there's a pot of coffee in the Ulysses, though!" Rob cried out as Abner approached.

"I just bought that keg a week ago! Do I need to enforce rations like the British Navy did for rum?"

"This isn't bad, Abe..." Claus said as he handed him a pint of poontrip. "I think Rob's had one too many." Abner grabbed the mug of ice-cold ale and drained it immediately. The heat of the day was dissipating along with Abner's thirst. A smile grew on his face as it did on the others. They put in a hard day together and were thankful to be in each other's company.

"Any of you have an enzyme pill for this?" Abner gestured with his cup, remembering the dangers of drinking poontrip without the supplement needed for the E-Tollian brew.

"Abe, you forget, we don't need it." Flip replied, with a ribbing smile.

"Ah, I forget, you're not human! Hard to believe I could forget!" He responded with equal sarcasm.

"I'm not so sure you'll smell human by the end of the night, Abe!" Claus interjected as the rest guffawed. Abruptly, Abner's laughter stopped as he turned white.

"No! Not tonight, we need to go to the palace!"

"Shouldn't a-been so thirsty!" Responded Rob.

"We can let ya know how it went," Flip added dryly.

"Seriously! I don't know what to do! We're kinda like de facto diplomats." Abner began to panic. "The leadership from Jook-Sing said we probably wouldn't see any Crehlians. They just gave us the agreed-upon coordinates for these sites."

"Well, Abner, I could go in your stead if you like," Claus added reassuringly.

"Thanks, Claus but, I've already met them. I can't back out now."

"Well, you know all poontrip brews are different. I've heard some can take a few days for their reactions to show up without the enzyme." Rob responded with hopeful encouragement after seeing Abner was seriously concerned.

It was very infrequent for this band of friends to be in the company of royalty. Their office of Shǒuhù Zhě did require them to meet with government officials of Jook-Sing from time to time. The difference was that Jook-

Sing's government was made up of elected representatives who were, by law, unable to make a career out of their appointments. It was illegal to hold an office for longer than four years. Most government ministers agreed with Jook-Sing's honor affirming society. Honor was poured out to all as every member was made in the image of The Creator.

Coming into contact with the lux earlier in the day had already put Abner off balance. He stopped to consider his thoughts, and after remembering the details of the encounter, he made up his mind. The lux's personality seemed very similar to those at even the highest levels of the Jook-Sing government. There was an easy-going humility deep within him in sharp contrast to his and the entourage's blindingly beautiful exteriors. Abner would keep his word and go to the palace. He would hope against hope that the poontrip's effects upon human anatomy would be delayed or at least subtle enough not to be sensed by the Crehlians.

The following hour and a half spent waiting for a free shower and shave further prolonged the inevitable. Abner finished cleaning up, dressed and sat down in the ship's lounge with all but Bob. The group looked stunning dressed in their formal Shǒuhù Zhě attire. Bob entered the room and sat beside Abner, smacking him on the knee as he sat. The former glad to be amongst this admirable group of men. Claus spoke first,

"We should head out." All arose and made their way to the surface glider left for them by the Crehlian delegation from the morning's informal meeting.

The group climbed up and into the vehicle while noting its luxurious accommodation for twelve passengers. Flip decided to pilot the machine, sat down to familiarize himself with the controls. He instinctively engaged the engine, after which the ports closed. The fish-man gained the confidence to drive the apparatus by giving the craft's interface subtle commands forward, reverse, left, and right. He typed in the palace's coordinates and pointed it toward the desired destination while leaving the autopilot off. The glider sat upon six wheels, making the name "glider" a mystery until the journey began. The path ahead was anything but

a prepared road surface. It was a vast waste, riddled with deep ruts, erosion trenches, potholes, and various sizes of rocks. They experienced that being within the vehicle erased the effect of everything the machine encountered. Its computer-controlled suspension and the electronically sound dampened cabin allowed for a quiet conversation with tea using fine china if desired while traveling at speeds above 200

MPH. Outside the cabin, the force field protected the glider from all debris while having the added effect of reinforcing the suspension system. They truly felt as though they were gliding above the surface of the desert. A half-hour elapsed as they began to see the palace in the distance.

The wasteland gave way to gradual patches of green. The grassland patches mixed in with divisions of clay and rocks made a beautiful site from the equivalent daylight power emitted from the glider's lamps. A road entrance funneled them toward civilization. The grasslands on either side of the road then began to be mixed with small trees similar to pines. A brilliant red soil delightfully complemented the grass, brown bark, and greenery of the trees. Then in the distance, the evening sky was contrasted with the small Crehlian town of Call's brilliance. Its lights ablaze beyond anything they had ever seen. Seen at the top of the tallest hill of Call sat the seat of power on Crehl. The Palace of Call.

Like a multicolored jewel, the palace was painted with colored light. Its walls illuminated as were the lamps emanating from every window and exterior lamp post. Like a painting, its only rival was those within its borders. The glider slowed instinctively to a prudent velocity.

It descended into a valley that at once obscured the view of Call and its palace. The occupants of the vehicle curiously shared a similar feeling of both abandonment and anticipation to see the glorious sight they knew was just ahead of them. Coming to the next hill's crest, around a bend, they once again beheld Call from their righthand windows. The view became magnified in brilliance.

Luxury

Flip made his final right turn to the long drive leading to the palace entrance. It, too, was lined with the most beautifully groomed examples of the familiar trees and grass amongst rich red soil. The driveway weaved amongst trees and valleys that heightened the allurement of the destination. The last mile of road was a straight arrow shot toward the front entrance of the royal residence. Lining the path on either side was a line of the familiar trees with fields of artistically scythed grass fields. The field's design, while intricate, was a blurred curiosity from the glider's windows. They were, like the palace, illuminated with artificial lights. The freshly combed white pea gravel landing was before them. Flip brought the glider to the front entrance as several footmen rushed from their posts to greet them. Opening the vehicle's doors, the servants welcomed the Shǒuhù Zhě with a mutual fascination with their appearances.

The group was led into The Great Hall as the Lux was informed of their arrival. The hall was filled with columns approximately twenty feet high. The ceiling lined with an aromatic wood that Abner assumed was sourced from the trees growing in abundance nearby. At about forty feet wide by sixty feet long, the hall lived up to its name. On either side upon its walls hung tapestries that though abstract, seemed to have a personal significance, somehow. The group of men wandered The Great Hall exploring the statues and artwork displayed when the Lux arrived. He made his way toward Abner as he was inspecting one of the tapestries.

"You know they are linked to us," he said with gentle authority. "This one is of my grandfather's legacy." Abner, slightly startled out of his concentration upon the finely detailed artwork.

"Oh, I'm sorry, Sir..ah... Your Honor. I didn't hear you."

"Please, just call me Aeq! I abhor how those with title demand others to subordinate themselves. I have no need to display my authority. I sense a great honor present in both you and your companions." He added with a smile, "Just Aeq!" As the Lux spoke, the great hall began to fill with the aroma of a deliciously spiced meal.

"Aeq, as long as you put it that way, I will try." Abner was thoroughly trapped by his natural desire to bow to this being. It was uncanny how the Lux's presence filled the hall with almost tactile electricity. The powerful smells from the kitchen, coupled with the sight of the Lux before him, was almost overwhelming. He wrestled against his instinct while trying to concentrate on something else, asked, "Aeq, is there a queen?"

"Abner, my queen or Lucerna is away on the other side of the planet, hunting valken. She is a gifted archer. It is her custom to spend a few weeks this time of year as they are in season. She is known as Lucerna Ignis and my greatest treasure." The head servant approached the Lux and whispered something to him at which, the Lux turned with excitement and proclaimed to all within the hall, "Our feast awaits! Please follow me to the dining hall!"

The great hall was filled with a savory smell of something beyond comprehension. It effect akin to the excitement a child would get before entering an amusement park. The dining room table was appointed with the most delicate china and golden flatware. They were seated. Large goblets at each place setting were filled with wine. Salads were offered of the most delicate greenery. A garden of Eden covered each plate. The dressings and cheeses accompanied their dish to perfection. Baskets overflowed with loaves similar to French bread baked to a golden brown. Each course that followed bore witness to the smell that had permeated the great hall earlier in its seasoning. There was a curry-like dish. The following was a roast with tuber-like vegetables. They were informed that this was valken, a beast similar to the impala of earth. The Lux reported to all of his Lucerne's skill as an archer to take down the nimble-footed valken. As the evening elapsed, the Lux asked many questions of the group. They had not outrun the fame of the Dirtstar conflict even in this remote location.

"So, you say it is true that ale was used against those infected?" The Lux inquired.

"Well, not exactly against them, more like it cured them," Rob explained. "We've come to understand those infected were hosts for a kind of super-yeast."

"So, similarly to all of you who were transformed, this yeast was as well?"

"Yes, although it didn't receive a body until finding a host." Clause added.

"Fascinating!" the Lux leaned back in his chair in contemplation, "I agreed to ally our world to yours in this crisis, yet, I was still a bit fuzzy on these points. It was obviously not eradicated completely. Do you know of its remanent source?"

"In all honesty, we've been just trying to contain what we can so far."

Across the table came the roar of Rob's voice during a poorly timed silence within the din of the party. While in mid yell to one of the Lux's entourage, the former donut's face was filled with embarrassment as he asked, "Why do your people look like angels?" The Lux sensed that the gaff's awkwardness was rapidly traveling through all of his guest's faces. He interjected, while quickly removing his upper garments. The sight, though designed in his mind to be equally awkward, had the desired effect that the Lux had hoped. No longer only his face and hands on display, they, along with his upper torso, commanded the visitors' attention.

"This, my friends, is why we of Crehl do not leave our homeworld. We are cursed with overwhelming beauty." The Lux's body was resplendent with refined detailed design. It was an abstract rendering of the man's life from birth interpreted by The Creator. "Long ago, our fathers were arrogant, self-absorbed people. Over the centuries, our culture degraded into chaos. The Creator revealed to one of our leaders that our people would be shown humility. Our children began to be born differently than their parents. They were the first Praeclarus. The generation who bore these children were cast into shame at the sight of their appearance in comparison. The Creator's rebuke was accepted, and they taught their offspring to worship The Creator only from that point onward. We, the Praeclarus, though grateful for our features, count them as a holy gift from God. We can discern his hand upon all of His creation and honor that work above our own appearance." The entire room fell utterly silent in reverence of the impact of the Lux's words after which, he lightheartedly called out, "How bout' desert?" He quickly covered himself and sat awaiting the next distraction needed to return equality amongst the room.

The servants brought in the deserts and a coffee-like drink. It was a shift in gears culinarily. It came composed of three courses with equally powerful fragrances to that of the dinner. The first a deliciously light ice cream-like dish with a red and gold fruit unlike any they had ever tasted. The next course was a rich dish that reminded all of a chocolate cake. The finale was served, a minty pudding that seemed to add an exclamation point to the entire meal. Bellies were full as conversations were winding down.

The party walked out to the balcony overlooking the brilliant fields of mown grass before the palace. The lights from the castle illuminated the area for miles, and they were able to discern the pattern clearly from this vantage as the image of a racing valken. The sight highlighted the Lux's eloquent words as a gentle warm breeze moved through the group.

"I cannot say how much we all appreciate your hospitality Aeq. You have given us a lifetime memory." Abner offered, as he shook the Lux's hand in farewell.

"You are most welcome, my friend. Please come again before you leave our world. We would like to spend more time with all of you."

The Shǒuhù Zhě made their way back to the glider and the Ulysses, as the Lux turned and spoke to the head servant.

"Mactus, please inquire of the chef, a concern. There was a strong odor within one of the dishes. I'm not sure which. Subtle yet, it smelled like a wet lojf! I'm just hoping we didn't serve anything rancid to our guests."

Once gathered together within the glider and out of sight of the palace, Clause yelled out,

"Quick! Open the windows! I'm dying! The group began to gag and cough for effect as the sweet breezes of the Crehlian fields replaced Abner's foul perspiration.

Division and Multiplication

Major Zhi sat in his quarters, sensing
something other than the darkness The
Collective provided. There was a quality of
light involved with whatever it was that
seemed to burn through that darkness. Though
faint, it was unable to be overpowered even by
"The Call" within himself. "The Call" had
become an obsession, darkness within the
dark. A hiding place, a way to make sure his
consciousness was irrelevant. There were
times when he was suddenly lucid like this
moment. It was much easier to avoid reality
and be drawn by "The Call" into oblivion.

"The Call" promised different things to
different hosts. The Collective's manipulation
of its cult was exhaustive in its variables. To
one, the promise of violence, to another, glory.
The gifts were endless. Many merely desired
the escape of numbing darkness, unable to
deal with their failure.

The light, as stated earlier, was a glimmer
through the blackness. Faint yet, this time, it

seemed to be tuned to something Liu had not experienced in ages. Hope.

Ludicrous- he thought. There is no hope for me. Liu was adamant as truth flowing within himself. He knew his betrayal of his country, family name, and his own life was absolute. The justice that had deposited him wherever he was now was warranted. Momentarily he almost pondered,

Where am I anyway? The despondency returned as he dropped the thought, and yet, the light was still there. It moved upon him once again, becoming brighter while hidden from The Collective's sight or understanding.

The glimmer reminded him of a Truth he had pushed off as a young man. The promise made by The Creator was never to leave. As a young man, he cared little for what he considered words used by men to manipulate the masses and rejected this Truth. The Truth had little regard for the way it was distorted by humanity. Neither did it regard the decision of a foolish young man. It remained the Truth. The words stayed faithful until needed. They were, after all, rooted in the good heart of The Eternal One. The self-imposed power of "The Call" was diminished within him today as this glimmer of light pierced the darkness around him.

It must have been the fact that Jenny and Cedric were interacting with a hive mind that

they were able to influence The Collective.
They were shielded from its perception while
infiltrating The Yeasts through their captive,
the connected host prisoner on Jook-Sing. It
needed to be a subtle nudge to keep from the
entity's discernment. They tested their theory
cautiously at first after entering The
Collective's thought processes. After entry,
both stepped back consciously, making eye
contact with each other, Cedric informed,
    "We've got to be careful here. This is like
disarming a time bomb. Control your thoughts.
We don't want for The Collective to have
access to us while we're in there!"
Jenny hesitated inwardly with fear while
knowing a need for their combined action in
this exercise.
    "Are you okay?"
The eflume empathetically questioned as he
suppressed his doglike need to attack in order
to protect her. Jenny was the perfect
counterpart, a reserve to his aggression. They
braced themselves and reentered The
Collective.
    Jenny and Cedric were caught unawares of
Major Zhi's struggle. While within The
Collective, they merely paused and began to
pray to The Creator for a way to release the
hosts and for their own protection. The effect
from within the enemy's camp caused a short
circuit like effect within the control of The

Collective. Every host aboard The Hydra began to question once again. The guidance of The Yeasts was temporarily disconnected for all but The Monster, his twelve, and the remaining Quandrosite zealots to "The Call" who remained on board.

The Collective, sensing it was losing control over its subjects, turned up its influence. On a cellular level, The Yeasts began to multiply within every host. The Hive Mind began to condense like a clot within the minds of every host under its influence.

Hidden in Plain Sight

The Hydra appeared once again above the skyline towers of New Seattle. Like an evil piñata, it hung in the sky above the Capitol building known as The House of Swords. It had somehow evaded all long and short-range sensors. Even Jook-Sing's secondary antiquated radar systems used as a failsafe failed. It hovered over the seat of power, taunting like a cat toy waiting to be noticed. The Collective was pleased that its state-of-the-art ghosting systems had proven to be worth the extra time to develop.

The guards posted on the roof had been performing their duties as trained, scanning the city streets and buildings. Preparing for an undetected threat from above never occurred to them. The Collective, within the Hydra engaged in silent mode, drew great enjoyment from this game as time elapsed. The sun rising above the islands in the bay had illuminated wisps of cloud, causing vibrant colors to appear in the sky. As the guards were admiring creation, they both looked up to see the hushed shape of the warship. From three hundred feet above them, the Yeasts roared with laughter through every host within the ship. The guards rushed for shelter in vain as the gunner host within his turret purposely spent an overabundance of rounds on his targets. The House of Swords erupted with alarm as the Hydra slowly descended to its roof. The enemy ship deposited a troop of fifty Quandrosite soldiers, all loyal to "The Call." Like guerrillas waiting to strike as the Jiàn Guard began to arrive at the rooftop, they fanned out. The Jiàn Guard or Jiàn Wèi had been chosen from the ranks of the Róngyù Shǒuhù Zhě to protect the capitol and its officials over a century ago.

Once laying its spawn, the Hydra rotated its path slightly to engage the light-duty fighters heading toward it. The otherworldly sounds once again began to emanate within its belly before the amplified blast pulsed like focused lightning toward the squadron of twenty fighters. Once the light dissipated, less than half remained as the remnant performed evasive maneuvers and continued their alternate flight paths. The weapon within the Hydra began to recharge as the hosts within their turrets fired conventional weapons toward the incoming ships.

The Collective commanded the hosts who were manning the KP weapon to fire. The weapon fired, the unseen particle traveling at supersonic speed, impacted the nearest fighter as it was removed entirely from the sky. Like the lightning weapon, the KP weapon, now in recharge sequence, was dormant.

Unexpectedly, a missile fired from one of the fighters had made it through and struck home. It had, by providence, hit the belly of the Hydra in the exact location of the KP weapon's power plant. Without knowledge of this fact, the pilot celebrated the hit as the explosion erupted from within the Hydra. The terror of the KP system had ended. Those outside of the Hydra were unaware of this blessing. Its most dangerous teeth were shattered.

The Collective, enraged, ordered all battle stations to fire as the ship rose and banked to port while engaging its ALS drives. The wake of its maneuver blew off the sword of the statue mounted atop the building. The thirty-foot sword fell to the rooftop, impaling a Quandrosite troop before stabbing into the roof and top two floors of the building.

The Hydra was gone. It had abandoned its Quandrosite troops and was in retreat while assessing damages. Guilty of a neophyte error, The Collective began to fulminate vocally against itself. Every host started yelling with rage within the ship, producing a cacophony of strife.

The infiltration had been almost perfect. Perfect would have been just thirty minutes earlier to prepare for and prevent the Hydra's attack. They were quick on their cerebral "feet" after breaking into the thought processes of The Collective. Cedric suggested to Jenny that they merely push the hive mind to overlook a primary step in preparing for its attack by nothing more than a distraction. Missing the small detail of the initiation of the ship's defensive shields was more than enough. It affected The Collective, like someone without enough sleep or lack of morning coffee. It was perfect. Everything hinged upon a barrage of questions and insults aimed at The Collective through the captive host. Cedric gave the signal to Claus, who was happy to comply. He posed inquires like: "Do you know the death toll associated with humanity's countless loaves of bread?" or "Did you know your kind was used as a metaphor by The Creator as He walked with His disciples throughout the land of Israel? He equated (the yeast of the Pharisees) to hypocrisy!" The Collective had spiraled out of control within this host while it was conducting a significant military operation.

The Yeasts began suspecting its host captive on Jook-Sing had something to do with its failure. The oppressor ran the host down without mercy. There was no difference whether or not it had an audience. The host was left in a cell, unable to use the bed provided. The Yeasts wouldn't allow it to eat or drink either. Days elapsed as the discourse continued around the clock with and without an audience. The Shǒuhù Zhě were forced to end all questioning due to the host's health. A treatment specially formulated by Nomar Eleeskee was provided. The host was then "baptized" while still in a near coma state. The ale-bath eventually eradicated all trace of The Yeasts within the Quandrosite's frail carcass. He revived slightly in what appeared to be a conflicted state between relief and a terror fueled failure.

After a week in the hospital, the host named himself as Vernon Filet. The data records of Quandros confirmed this truth along with another curious side-note. This man was a first cousin to Marcus Filet. Though his appearance was a slight tell, his character did resemble the Marcus Filet of years past. It was an odd coincidence.

"I caught nothing from The Collective on their relation. I would think we would have, especially knowing The Yeasts were unaware of our probing." Jenny blurted out to Cedric, Claus, and Danielle. "I've gotta say that doesn't make me any more comfortable with this!"

"We're gonna have trust providence that this is just quirky parallelism," Cedric said after a long pause. The four investigators sat at the table in silence as a circumspect hush rested upon them.

Boots on the Ground

The Quandrosite troops still tethered to The Collective fanned out within The House of Swords as the Hydra roared away in retreat. Like a disease, they infiltrated the building, killing as many inhabitants as possible. The enemy worked with stealth and surprise, implanting themselves with skill and cunning. The Jiàn Guard commander called upon Jelly to rally the elite Shǒuhù Zhě of the junxio to assist in defense of the Capitol. Jelly ran to Jenny and Cedric before leaving for the Capitol while they were still within The Collective. Jenny, sensing Jelly's presence, signaled to Cedric to leave.

"There's been an attack on The House of Swords!" Jelly exclaimed, "We need to go there now!" The Collective speaking through the Quandrosite host, Vernon Filet, smiled, sensing their pain, calmly stated,

"Please come, yes, join us at the capitol for your deaths."

Fifteen minutes elapsed as the Shǒuhù Zhě of the junxio, including several of its retired elders, assembled in the House of Swords' courtyard. While in transit, each member was briefed through their comm link by the Jiàn Guard commander Jacon Xian. Cedric and Jenny looked at each other, knowing their infiltration of The Collective had been a success. The Hydra's shields were down during the battle allowing substantial damage before its retreat. Thankful for the win, they steeled themselves for this next battle beyond the cerebral.

Commander Xian directed the Shǒuhù Zhě to join the Jiàn guard in rooting out the Capitol's infection. Once receiving direction, each member was given the new anti-DDM weapons developed by Professors Lantooto and Kackman. They rushed to the supply crates being unloaded from the transport truck that arrived minutes after them. All obtained a belt of anti-DDM gas grenades and an assault weapon loaded with the new serum in dart form. All stormed into the building at its various entrances and fanned out within the levels to engage the enemy.

Upon entry into the building's centrally-located grand colonnade, the Shǒuhù Zhě fanned out amongst the thirty-foot columns that filled the hall. All around lay the bodies of unsuspecting civilian casualties. Their deaths a brutal disrespect of life and all held to be known as good. These innocents lay strewn throughout the complex. The knowledge that these were created in the image of God being the fuel behind their debasing deaths. Abner directed the teams of four to proceed into the building. The Shǒuhù Zhě's training kicked in as they redirected powerful emotions toward completing the task at hand. They flowed like rushing water within and beyond the forest of marble into every corner of the Capitol.

Team one consisted of Jenny, Abner, Louie, and Maude. The hallway to the south of the grand colonnade was lined with doors to legislator's offices every fifteen feet. Trying hard to distract her own emotions, Maude whispered to Louie,

"This is like rooting out a roach infestation."

"Roaches... my least favorite animal", he whispered back.

"They're not animals, Louie. They're insects." She whispered with a mock air of disdain to her neanderthal partner.

"I thought insects were animals. Are you sure ya know what your talkin' bout?"

"Ah, never mind, you could never understand having a head full of lemon jelly."

"It's a good thing I like cinnamon."

They began clearing offices as they proceeded down the hall. Halfway down the corridor, a door exploded open as each team member moved against the walls on either side. Two Quandrosites began spraying down the passage with automatic gunfire as they entered the opposite office space. Abner entered the nearest office and called others to follow. He was immediately grabbed from behind in a chokehold by a large Quandrosite. Before the others could assist, Abner struggled to reach the anti-DDM dart in his belt. Within the hallway, working against his assailant, he quickly walked up the opposing wall and flipped to the Quandrosite's back as he plunged the anti-DDM and sedative filled projectile into the man's neck. The Quandrosite went limp, slumping to the ground as the chemicals began to surge through his bloodstream.

The anti-DDM compound, once entering the host's body, began to encounter The Yeasts within the man's blood. The individual yeast cells initially inspected the intruding chemicals with curiosity, noting them to be different from anything they had ever encountered. Apart from sensing a note of pain from the host, the chemical seemed to be inert as it was spread to the body's entire anatomy. Once equally dispersed, the time-release coating upon both portions of the two-part concoction dissolved. Like a timed explosion, the chemicals mixed, rupturing the sentient elements of The Yeast's DNA within the host.

Though sedated, the effect caused a visible change in the Quandrosite's eyes. Immediately, The Collective lost all contact with this host. He sat on the floor, confused. The Call within him struggled, knowing its shepherd was missing. He passed out partially due to sedation but mainly because of the shock of abandonment. He now was merely a terrorist with a blood born yeast infection, snoring in the hallway.

"Dang, that was close," Louie whispered. Abner held up his finger to his mouth for silence as the four continued to clear the offices. Three more doors revealed empty rooms. Before they reached the next door, it burst open as ten Quandrosites rushed the hall. Maude threw an anti-DDM grenade at the quickly growing mob twenty-five yards opposite of the four. They attempted to scatter, two collided, knocking themselves out within the cloud of gas. The others rushed the four with knives drawn. Jenny and Abner ran to meet them, swords in hand. The anti-DDM gas began to take hold of their assailants, causing a momentary lapse of judgment for the first row of five Quandrosites. They lashed out with their weapons a full foot short of their targets. The gas completed its work as the untethered and confused enemies worked to stay focused. The gas grenades lacked the sedative, allowing the men to remain alert while in their baffled condition. All four, freed of The Collective yet, still firmly within The Call's influence, lunged once again at Jenny and Abner.

Jenny allowed the closest thrust to pass her by as she grabbed hold of the man's arm, using his momentum to flip him. He bounded up immediately, turning his head slightly to watch Abner's blade hammer down with a precision stroke that removed his left arm at the shoulder. He was literally dis-armed. The man's adrenaline kicked in even more while fumbling for his pistol positioned for his missing arm. He managed to unbutton the holster just as the shock kicked in due to his injuries. The man fell in a limp pile as the next Quandrosite took his place. The hallway was a blur with the four Shǒuhù Zhě cutting down the insurgents before them. Maude, having trained like her companions with many forms of martial arts, changed her styles rapidly. She settled upon the Krav Maga form as the current Quandrosite engaged had nearly knocked her to the ground. She knew deep within her training that once the enemy has you on the floor, your vulnerability is increased substantially. The following knife laden lunge by the evil man was redirected by Maude's quick reflexes. She had disarmed the attacker and, with the same circular motion, plunged the long knife down through his collar bone into his heart. Turning quickly to the right, she thrust the blade through one temple and out the other of the commando attempting to assist the one fallen before her. The four remaining Quandrosites stopped as they watched their commander collapse before her. All four threw their weapons down in surrender. Whether this was cowardice or wisdom, the Quandrosites were less effective without the tie to The Collective. The captives were secured, and the four continued to clear the House of Swords along with the other teams.

The Fallen Sword

The battle eventually concentrated on the top floor of the building. Fifteen or so of the remaining terrorists had taken twenty captives within the same room that had been thrust through by the decorative sword earlier in the day. The gleaming gold blade passed from the ceiling to where the tip entered deep into the floor in the center of the room. On the floor lay the corpses of the first twelve hostages. The Quandrosites, fueled by the rage of The Collective, had been throwing their prisoners at the fallen blade. Bifurcated and beheaded bodies lay opposite the trajectory of the hysterical terrorists.

Those first to enter the room cast in their remaining gas grenades. The effect was immediate yet, once again, The Call, was still intact as the fanatic Quandrosites carried on their twisted evil with drunken abandon. The remaining hostages huddled together behind them, forced to watch this carnival of carnage.

Cedric bounded into the room, thinking his form would be a surprise to the assailants within. His seven-hundred-pound bulk flashed like lightning from the room's entrance to the first five Quandrosites. Massive forearms flashed out with paws brandishing their enormous claws. All five men were immediately torn to pieces and cast in all directions as the eflume's rage erupted after seeing the dead captives. He spun around again, his corded coat looking like a hurricane changing direction toward the next row of Quandrosites. Their mouths were agape at this point, arms like dead fish at their sides.

Behind these men, the remainder of the Quandrosite troops readied their weapons and trained them on this new threat. They had no idea what this beast was or was able to do. Without any other ideas, they began to fire wildly upon the animal. Cedric was cerebrally linked to each of those about to fire upon him. It appeared to everyone who witnessed the incident firsthand that the eflume was like a ghost. He moved through the automatic gunfire as though it was passing through him without effect. Every synapse within his mind was finely tuned while he dodged and weaved past the thunderous barrage before him. Grasping the nearest Quandrosite, he used first as a shield, then as a projectile. Rising on his back legs, he threw the Quandrosite shield down from his full height of twelve feet. The

power behind this action toppled over eight
terrorists.
Danielle, Jelly, and Flip burst into the room
while Cedric's diversion was still in play.
Danielle, first at Cedric's side, within a split
second ascertained whether or not the
assailants would surrender. The remaining
killers bounded up once again in blind
adherence to "The Call." The first to engage,
figuring the cyborg to be a soft target, slashed
out with his battle-ax. Danielle multitasked,
her mind calculated thrust, trajectories, angles,
the man's biology, and the weapon's design
then moved just out of the ax's downward
path. At the optimal millisecond, her
lightning-fast reflexes engaged her mechanical
arm. In a motion too swift to discern, her arm
shot out, hand grasping the ax handle just
below its blade. She redirected the downward
circular motion. It was too late for the
Quandrosite to let go of the weapon as he was
hurled toward the gigantic fallen sword and
severed in two. His fate was reciprocated as he
had
instigated the similar deaths of his hostages.
　　Flip joined the fray just after Danielle. A
large Quandrosite attempted to knock him
down. Flip's unique fighting nature engaged as
the fish-man "flipped" out of his way only to
return the action. He rushed the enemy below
his center of gravity. The Quandrosite fell over

and bounced back up like a gymnast. Flip now with sword in hand, exchanged sword parries with the large man. At once, he received a gash on the left side of his forehead. The blood began to flow into his left eye. His training ignited once again to fend off the distraction as adrenaline coursed through his frame. Flip, slashed high as a distraction then, low at the enemy's leg. This distraction opened the path for Flip's blade to decapitate his adversary.

The elderly Shǒuhù Zhě master, Martin Lim, known by his nickname "Iron Ankle", continued the search for the remaining Quandrosites on the third floor of The House of Swords. He and his team lead by Loaf entered a large auditorium and fanned out toward the stage. A group of ten Quandrosites erupted from behind the rear curtains toward the Shǒuhù Zhě as the group ascended the platform.

Iron Ankle engaged two attackers as they lunged toward him, their blades a blur. At once, he was invisible. His movement too rapid to be seen. The master's age vanished before them as he flew through the air with a scissor like action to the heads of his foes. His ankles, a death blow to their skulls. Like a feather, the octogenarian alighted to the floor as the Quandrosites fell with a thunderous clap to the wood beneath them.

Simultaneously on the opposite side of the stage the drama continued. Loaf and Basir confronted five attackers emerging from the back of the stage. Loaf as pure muscle, after bounding to the stage deck made several powerful strides toward the enemies and immediately tucked into a forward roll. The stunned expressions of the Quandrosites was quickly obscured by his impact on the two men in closest vicinity to each other. Knocked down like bowling pins, each hitting their heads against the other on the way down before the oakwood floor had its say. The four men, two on either side of the stage produced a drum roll effect with their almost perfectly timed gravity fueled head impacts.

The three Quandrosites before Basir began a show of intimidation. Their swords flashed in unison with the three's perfectly timed movements. Each warrior's body moving machine-like with the man beside him. Basir advanced without hesitation, curved scimitar in hand. He began his attack toward the center adversary. His diagonal downward swipe at the nearest target was rewarded with a graze to the cheek of the man. Basir allowed his momentum to rotate his body as all three men drew closer, their blades singing. The Whirling Dervish Persian's form recalled his previous donut form. The color of his clothes and small turban blurring with the speed of his rotation. With each turn-about, his head locked to prevent loss of balance while his eyes focused to their targets. While rotating, the scimitar emerged, first defensively blocking blows followed by a centrifugal force fueled slash that took down all three like blades of unwanted grass.

The remaining three Quandrosites dropped their weapons and lay prone upon the stage. These men were content to encounter the oakwood deck in a more peaceful way. They felt a sense of relief after the grenade laden gas had taken effect just before the Shǒuhù Zhě's performance had begun. Each was now a fan.

The Ghost and the Machine

Marcus was starting to get a handle on his abilities to navigate the Christy shaped quantum portals. The reset had rejoined him with FM. Immediately after his grief-filled plunge into the quantum realms, his own consciousness in the form of FM rejoined him. Curiously, in a flash, his grief was changed to resolve. He had already lived through the grief FM encountered and was rejoined with that portion of himself. The switch was like a lightning bolt. He was reminded of The Creator, who is inside and outside of time and matter. Time jumping was becoming a novelty to Marcus yet, pondering The Creator's mastery was overwhelming. He was awestruck by how his own experience in this realm was like an ant navigating the heavens or like the Apostle Peter walking on water. The Creator, unbound by His creation, would view Marcus' progress as arduous.

It took him a few misfired attempts to locate the correct time, but he exited the portal and made his way to the junxio. Disembodied once again, he tried to find Cedric or Jenny. He walked through the door of the school to Jenny's surprise.

"I suspected you might walk through the door again, Marc! Are you okay?"

"I'm fine, Jenny, I'm guessing everything is as FM predicted?"

"Well, you should know, both of you have been missing since the attack. As far as FM's warnings, there are slight details that are different, but, On the whole, everything is as he- you said it would be. This is weird, huh?"

"Yeah, try being the one it happened to."

"I can't imagine. You don't seem to be taking it too bad."

"I wonder if FM has something to do with it. It's as though the things he tried to explain, down to the emotional aspects of the experiences he went through, immediately made sense to me after dropping into the portal for the first time." Marcus explained as he focused on Jenny. She smiled, knowing he was comforted by their friendship.

"Well, I'm thinking we can put you to work! There may be a way we can team you up with Danielle. I'm hopeful both of you may be able to locate Christy together." Jenny spent time with Marcus explaining the curious gifts Danielle had been given. She discussed her experiences with SNAM and her hopes of the two teaming up as a quantum jumping search and rescue team.

Another two weeks passed. Marcus once again became accustomed to being disembodied. He learned to write quickly on his notepad to be able to stay connected to his family. The floating pen, furiously working its pad, became a fascinating novelty at the junxio. He longed to speak verbally again and to be heard. This form of isolation, while tolerable, was annoying.

With Jenny's engineering abilities and collaboration with Danielle's SNAM, a communication tool was produced. Danielle was finally given a way to communicate with Marcus. They were both given specially designed components of the instrument. Marcus was able to wear the communication device on his head. A sensor was placed upon his right temple to interpret his inanimate brainwaves and transmit them directly to Danielle's SNAM brain. They were a bizarre sight as the two left the junxio- a cyborg and a headset floating at her side.

Marcus tried out his end of the comm.

"Danielle, I know this is odd for you but, I am so thankful you are the one helping me to find Christy."

"Marc, you know how much I love that girl. You two are perfect. I've been a mess since the two of you've been gone. Don't worry. I've been getting used to my SNAM. I have hope that won't go away." Danielle's voice was relayed back to Marcus with an oddly robotic tone while transmitted through her SNAM as she spoke her reply.

SNAM was interpreting and analyzing every movement and vocal intonation of their conversation while simultaneously monitoring quantum variants as the two walked back to the invisible Christine shaped hole outside the restaurant where Marcus' latest emergence had occurred. In the street, the monument to his loss and hope blazed before him. Danielle walked up to it, nearly placing her foot into the abyss. Marcus pulled her back from the brink, not remembering this portal was closed to those within this time-dimension.

"What!" Danielle proclaimed while startled at Marcus' detention.

"I'm so sorry, I forgot, you can't see it. If only there were a way for you to see what I can see!" Danielle suddenly had a vision within so quickly; she was unable to understand it. It was as though she knew her SNAM was working toward a rapid upgrade. Seconds elapsed, and she announced as to herself,

"There, can you see it now?" Both stopped, beholding the miracle the AI had accomplished. Danielle took a step backward in awe of what was before her. As though answering herself, she replied,

"Yeah, dang, that's amazing. Terrifying Marc." She looked up at the floating headset that was at her side a second ago. Marcus was standing next to her, looking haggard yet, not without hope as he looked at her smiling. He had no idea she could see him until their eyes met, and he knew he could be seen again. The feeling was akin to being rescued from a desert island. Danielle reached out her hand and grabbed his shoulder saying,

"We're gonna find her, Marc! I can taste it!"

I Am Your Father

Colonel Ramar Gleek rocketed past in his fighter. Loaf in The Ulysses took his position just behind him on the starboard side. The remainder of the squadron followed closely on either flank. The following two weeks after the attack upon The House of Swords had been torturous while waiting in the barracks upon Crehl. They had just received orders from Jook-Sing of the Hydra's location. Fortunately, during the previous week's attack, a projectile homing beacon was fired at the enemy's ship. The device provided new eyes to the leaders within the crippled House of Swords.

Colonel Gleek, the older warrior, well beyond retirement, had been preparing his fleet composed of an alliance between the Jook-Sing navy, the Commonwealth, the Crehl Air, and Space Defense, and, to everyone's surprise, the Dejeali Space Force. The Crehli government had quickly approved the needed request for additional airbases in various locations on their planet's surface to support the Alliance.

The Colonel chuckled to himself while calling out to his offspring. Inwardly, enjoying the novelty of having one of the strangest family members known in creation.

"Sergeant Gleek, you're gonna have to keep up if you wanna see some action today!"

Loaf, having met his father/DNA donor two years past, had no difficulty seeing resemblances in his character to that of the Colonel. He had grown to have a deep fondness for his father, embracing every aspect of their relationship. Loaf was eager to be entrusted with the wisdom his architect shared.

Having his father's natural abilities was not the same as experience. Though not officially part of any military, Loaf was a Shǒuhù Zhě; therefore, the Colonel had given him the honorary title of Sergeant. In reality, the Colonel knowing Loaf's abilities as a pilot could have granted a higher title. He realized Loaf's interest in titles was weak and decided upon Sergeant to avoid any strife amongst the rank and file.

"I'm right on your tail Old Man! It's a good thing I'm on your side, or you'd be meeting your maker!" The Colonel chuckled in reply as he engaged his fighter's ALS drive and vanished for a brief moment. Loaf also initiated the Ulysses' ALS drive along with the remaining fleet at his stern, port, and starboard sides. The entire fleet was now within ALS as a unit. The comm crackled while within the light speed realm.

"One thing I've never thought to ask you, how do you feel about my love for meatloaf? It's still the only thing I know how to make." Came the ribbing banter from the Colonel.

"I eat meatloaf, Dad! Why would I have a problem with you loving something I love? Loaf responded sardonically to the Colonel.

"Don't you have a moral issue with that Son? I think that maybe a form of cannibalism."

"Well, you were formed from the dust of the Earth!" Loaf responded, his voice conveying a suppressed laugh.

"Yeah, I'll bite…"

"You've been eating my dust for the last two weeks, Sir." Loaf's smile was audible through the static of the comm.

"Well, we'll see about that, young man!"

A squadron of ten Dejeali fighters joined to the port and starboard of the two leaders and trailing back beyond the entire fleet to its aft. They appeared like a fleet of Bunyanesque fighters on either side of the fleet. Every pilot between these leviathans felt as though within a canyon while traveling at light speed.

"Bout' time, Ya'll showed up!" Colonel Gleek jested to the Dejeali fighters.

"We thought it might be fun for you to have some real power!" The Dejeali squadron commander joked. The jest, more of a statement of fact as just one Dejeali fighter, was close to half the size of a supermax freighter. What they lacked in stealth, these ships made up for in sheer size and physical armor. Their weapons systems were also in keeping with the scale of the machinery. On average, the pilots stood at a height of twenty feet. These ships accommodated the pilot and his weapons tech seated facing the tail. Visible through the squadron commander's canopy, the Dejeali pilot's huge smile brightened all within view.

The entire fleet began to arrive at the calculated location in a distant position near the planet Quandros. In rapid-fire succession, each ship came out of ALS while still in formation.

"There it is, opposite of the planet Sir!" came the voice of a radar tech onboard one of the fleet's jamming ships. "I've initiated radar stealth for the fleet, Sir."

"Confirmed Phillips, I see it too." addressing the fleet, "Gentlemen, on my command, I want a quick wave originating from north and south poles to the target from teams eight and eleven. Once engaged, the remaining teams need to proceed from opposite latitudes. The Dejeali forces should be last. I don't want to fill the airspace with too much hardware at once." Each ship confirmed the Colonel's orders. The fleet locked their position above Quandros.

All was still as each member called upon The Creator for protection and guidance. The situation was not a light matter. Every pilot was keenly aware of their need to spill enemy blood. Many imagined those aboard the Hydra, knowing these hosts, especially the Quandrosites, had families and friends who would not see them return. Even the knowledge of a willing heart did not deter this unearned empathy. Quandrosite history was taught to all involved. It was a civilization of harsh paradox, great selfishness, and sacrifice. A society leaning heavily upon the culture of "The Call." The general public and its elites relied upon "The Call" to secure the narcissism it enjoyed. "The Call" had permeated the norms of society. The system engaged everyone on either side of the divide, a justification toward the practice equaling that of religion. The gods of this world were the elites. They plied the masses with encouragement toward "The Call" in hypnotic reoccurrence.

All at once, the command exploded, "Teams eight and eleven…Go!" Barked Gleek, In the lead ship of team eight, engaged

his thrusters and flashed away from the fleet
with the remainder of teams eight and eleven.
"Backing teams... Go!"
The remaining ships exploded away from the
behemoths who waited for the Colonel to call
upon the Dejeali forces.

Time dragged on for the Dejeali crews.
They had anticipated a ten-minute wait,
maximum. The delay was close to twenty
minutes at this point. They had been
monitoring the chatter of their allies until the
main forces left them behind. Time elapsed
until their signals were blocked by the
jamming ships. Patience was a key character
asset to most Dejealis so, they waited.

Cornered

The Collective was preoccupied with various repairs to the Hydra's hull and weapons systems within the orbit of its ally, Quandros. The covenant between the government of this belligerent planet and The Collective was binding. It would eradicate any contingencies Quandros may attempt. The contract was signed in blood. As far as The Collective was concerned, this was a safe harbor. The detailed damage reports began filling the screens near key hosts as the Yeasts rested in a false sense of security

The KP weapon and its fortifications were obliterated beyond repair. It would have to be remanufactured from the ground up. The Collective began to eye Quandros as more than an ally after receiving the latest news. The planet had vast resources. Knowing the repairs and new manufacturing could be done in plain sight was a great desire for The Yeasts. Work could be completed in a fraction of the time it had taken while in hiding upon Tolkee.

Hosts were rushing around the Hydra, either performing various repairs or supporting those who were. The Collective being present within the thoughts of every member of the ship was focused. The result was not unlike a beehive.

All at once, the unimaginable occurred like multiple flashes of lightning. One by one, its enemy arrived within range of its destruction.

The damned humans! They're like an infected stain. The Collective cursed as every host's face became a twisted scowl in response to their lord sharing its emotions.

We'll see how they react to the full power of Quandros!

The Collective directed those at the helm to dive to the surface of the planet. As they maneuvered the descent, a missile was brought home to its target at the rear of the Hydra.

The Collective hailed the ground defenses of Quandros as it began passing through the atmosphere. Immediately, Quandros responded with surface to space missiles and railgun-fire upon the fleet as the Hydra escaped. Orbiting military satellites came online and began a barrage of laser defenses.

The fleet arrived in time to fire off a few volleys at the Hydra as it descended. Most of the missiles missed their mark and burned up in the planet's atmosphere. They then made half-hearted attempts to strike the forces on the surface yet, were unsuccessful. Most of the fleet turned back to rejoin the waiting Dejeali fighters. They had lost four soldiers and stopped to pick up the ejected pilots from their ship's debris fields.

In its haste, the Hydra's angle of descent was insufficient for optimal safety. Areas of the outer hull not covered in heat deflecting tiles began to glow cherry red. Just before passing the harshest point of reentry, those areas began to melt and further deform the starship's outer image. It found its landing pad within the specially built base just outside of the capitol. The ship touched down after-which, the mooring cleats laboriously locked to its deformed lashing anchor points.

The Hydra, now in its moorings, sat upon the surface of Quandros like a deformed cancer cell. Any projection of power or mastery of design was lost. Melting panels above the heat resistant tiles began to harden into new unintended forms. The ship now appeared like a symbol of the disease that it was.

The fleet worked hard in avoidance of the planet's defenses. They were still above the surface, like determined insects avoiding a flyswatter. Quandrosite forces and The Collective remaining aboard the Hydra rested once again, feeling untouchable. It grumbled vocally to itself,

"Human filth soon all will be absorbed. This game will end. We will be a god. All will serve The Collective. We feel it. We proclaim it will be done! They will no longer serve another. We will ascend above all. To think, they will no longer need to think apart from us. We will control reason, emotion, and the will of all. We will incorporate "The Call" into our seduction. They will be compelled to join us. For a little leaven works through the whole batch. They will have no desire to verify Truth, no need for resistance. Let us begin here on the planet Quandros. This population of double-minded fools will become a willing participant within Us. More worlds will follow, and there will be peace. For true peace is the destruction of chaos."

The Collective's thoughts, fueled by hatred and defeat, rambled on to itself like a cornered animal protecting its wounds. It chose to disregard the fact that the landfill incident had given it an intellect derived from the evil present within human DNA. In a sense, it was more human than its enemies. Soul-less, it lacked a conscience, allowing unbridled corruption. It had no desire to be introspective to this Truth, only to continue toward domination. It was uncanny how the yeast molecule's natural tendencies and man's fallen nature had similar yearnings. Both were occupied with spreading their desires, overtaking and feeding off of all in their path. They had no regard for what was left in their wake. Narcissism was a virtue, a fuel, a means toward the goal. It was The Collective's religion. The Collective had no regard for Truth. No need for any opposition, no observation of fact. It saw only a future filled with itself. The Yeasts allowed a tickle up the spine of the nearest host as it pondered its future, dominating all others and receiving their worship.

Colonel Gleek had decided to stave off the Dejeali forces for the time being. The Dejeali ships had the firepower to reach the surface of the planet. There was much to contemplate knowing Quandros was complicit in this struggle. The last thing anyone wanted was a ground assault. Colonel Gleek had the unhappy task of bringing this bad news of an infected Quandros to The House of Swords.

Failed Diplomacy

Once again, Colonel Gleek led the fleet to Quandros. Unlike the first sortie, this mission had amassed to include seventy percent of the allies' space going hardware. The fighters led the group into ALS as various forms of craft followed. There were fully occupied troop transports, fighters, hospital ships, and various support vessels to contribute to the assault upon Quandros including the patient Dejealis.

"Ready for another serving, Pops!" Loaf hailed the Colonel from the Ulysses through the static laden commlink within the ALS field.

"Y'all know meatloaf is comfort food, Loaf?"

"Yeah, your point?"

"I think Quandros is gonna have some digestive problems when they meet a meatloaf as old as you, Son!"

"Just keep eyes on your instruments, Pops. I don't think they'll have time to eat today!" Loaf shot back as the two chuckled.

The massive fleet dropped out of ALS within the Quandrosite atmosphere. The shock to the planet radiated in the sky for hundreds of miles in all directions. The sight and sound-evoked the fury of an atomic bomb's detonation. The allies took advantage of this complementary side-effect. The disturbance of their arrival had an EMP-like effect within the upper hemisphere of the planet.

The fleet began to disperse according to plan. Troop transports filled with soldiers from the Commonwealth, E-Toll, Dejeal, and Jook-Sing followed assigned coordinates to the surface. The shuttles that carried Shǒuhù Zhě, including the Ulysses, dove to their targeted locations at key positions of the city of Kjett.

Loaf made a steep dive to the E-Tollian embassy. He then engaged the anti-gravity drives as the crew dropped like a feather to the ground from ten feet above the surface. The Ulysses then shot back to the upper atmosphere like a patient chauffeur on high. Once reaching beyond the limits of the ground forces, Loaf locked in the hover mode.

"Be safe out there, Colonel. I want to see you make it back in one piece."

"Good thing that's coming from you and not me!" Colonel Gleek replied.

"Why's that?"

"One piece of meatloaf is never enough!" the Colonel replied with an exaggerated Texan accent, Loaf's response, an equally melodramatic groan.

At the E-Tollian embassy, Abner and his team, along with three more groups, each lead by Jelly, Louie, and Flip, fanned out in search of Ambassador Doncless. One by one, the guards fell as the forces of New Seattle silently immobilized them. These Quandrosite soldiers on loan from their government for the Ambassador's use proved to be less than effective in their vocation.

Jelly's team consisting of Maude, Layerie, Swaying Reed, and Basir, walked the staircase to the second floor. At the far end of the hallway before them were two guards deep in conversation while playing cards. Taking advantage of the adversary's focus, the team charged toward them like a rushing river. Both men rose in surprise just in time to see Swaying Reed's willow branch-like form strike. In the following days, they would argue about what happened. Both shared similar goose-egg knots on their heads. The details, apart from these physical reminders, were missing.

After neutralizing the guards, Jelly's team cautiously entered the residence level of the embassy. In the far corner of the room sat Doncless. His eyes were locked to the monitor while attempting to take in the details of the video feed, ignoring all commentary.

Dejeali warriors were streaming through the capitol city. Their forms needing little magnification, each man between twenty and thirty foot tall. Though Dejealis were known to be of noble character with a desire for peace without bloodshed, these soldiers caused panic in the streets. The propaganda machine of Quandros worked hard to change the obvious narrative.

He knew the Quandrosite media was nothing more than propaganda to fuel "The Call." It appeared his delicate dance with the devil would soon be over. The dance was never free yet, he had continually pushed the expected payment out of his mind until now. E-toll's Ambassador to Quandros had been rife with turmoil from the beginning. Like most politicians, he was willing to bend whichever way was necessary to satisfy both world's desires while attempting to benefit himself. Over the past twenty years, his office had been a reliable point of stability between two very different societies. All at once he saw everything disintegrating before his eyes.

Xytist Doncless began public service with the best of intentions. Descendant from an E-Tollian farming family, like most of his kind, he had greater aspirations than ortric farming. He worked his way up through the political sea of E-Toll, beginning at twelve years old as a page in the Senate. As a senator, his influence touched the majority of the political and bureaucratic worlds of his home planet before entering intergalactic diplomacy. Becoming a diplomat was the unexpected culmination of his life's aspirations. His experience as an ambassador was not without its setbacks. The most significant drawback being a physical disadvantage, the higher "G" loads present on the planets he visited. The hovercarts employed to allow for his mobility were a great help yet, an equal prison. The two months per year, vacation on E-Toll was heavenly. The last five years began to be filled with a longing for home more than any other desire. Doncless wanted for nothing. He was a wealthy man, accustomed to luxury. His life now in its sunset years, he realized his ambitions had robbed him of the best of life. Now, before him on the Quandros state-run news, an exit was forming in his heart and mind.

Startled by the group of phantom Shǒuhù Zhě, he quickly turned his head away from the tribulations on the screen to face uncertainty. He then recognized a few faces.

Could this be the answer to my hopes? Or justice for my crimes?

"Ambassador Doncless, we are here to evacuate you back to E-Toll." Jelly announced through winded breaths, "I apologize, Sir but, we have no more than five minutes for you to gather your belongings."

"You, Ma'am, are Jelly! I remember you. You are the latest shifu. I've been informed you are a famous teacher and an adept warrior. I read the account of how you neutralized your assassins during your own inauguration! You must understand, I have a special place in my heart for your group of friends. I was shocked at the news of the attack and relieved you were unharmed. I trust you received the letter I sent to the junxio after the incident?"

"Yes, I did, Sir. I do appreciate your words, but," Jelly's impatience lay just below the surface, "we really must go for the safety of all."

"Yes, of course, I feel as though angels are rescuing me. I'll get my bag. Everything else I'll need is on the Ulysses."

Jelly's team led the Ambassador down to the ship's moorage. The embassy was now secure as Doncless boarded his starship. Abner eyed the ship he and his friends had "borrowed" years ago with a renewed love for its form and the memories associated with it. He looked around to see his companions sharing similar expressions as they, too, viewed the ship.

School

Ambassador Doncless' Ulysses quickly rose above the embassy just out of the danger zone and immediately engaged full DLS. Though not a dangerous maneuver, the powerful effect reverberated for miles in every direction, both audibly and visually. The sky visibly waved in shock as the multifaceted sonic boom followed ten seconds afterward. The Shǒuhù Zhě teams, relieved, turned their attention toward locating the Hydra.

An excruciating ten minutes elapsed before the reconnaissance ships sent their reports to the rest of the fleet. Abner hailed Loaf piloting their Ulysses in the upper atmosphere.

"Loaf, jah get our target?"

"Yessir, received. I'm on my way to gather my chicks."

"See ya in a sec," Abner responded while scanning the Shǒuhù Zhě before him. He was well aware of the need for this operation, but it still didn't take his mind off the possibility of losing one of these valuable people. He had complete confidence in every one of them. It mattered very little that some started their existence without the human trait. Every one of them possessed the best qualities one could desire in a fellow warrior. These were not merely comrades, they were family.

Abner allowed his training to take over his thoughts. The goals of the mission would take precedence over emotion. Their values rooted in honor would guide him. Jenny walked up just before his focus was steeled. Knowing her husband to be an open book whether she was using her gifts or not, she rubbed his shoulder, saying,

"We can trust The Creator, Abe."

"I just let my mind wander a bit too much, Jen. We've been given so much. All of us know there's no guaranty any of us will make it home. It's pretty obvious we won't have a home if this plague continues."

"I agree." Jenny felt the weight of Abner's words flow over her. Her reaction was directed by wisdom obtained by experience. She could think of nothing else to say. She merely looked deep into his eyes before both allowed their training to focus their minds. Just then, the Ulysses arrived overhead and began its descent. Jenny allowed her sentimental thoughts back for a moment as the ship slowly rested on the tarmac.

Both first and second Ulysses had been within sight in the last half hour. The memories began to flood her heart. The questions Abner had just confronted came to her in power as recollections filled her mind like a cinema. The two ships were like an ark filled with beautiful things. Her mind quickly shot back to her days working in the facilities department on the Dirtstar. She already possessed a full life at that time. She would never have believed how life would play out from that point forward. The providence involved gave her no warnings. The endless days spent diagnosing issues with conveyor PLC's or sealing persistent micrometeorite hull breaches had come to an end without prior alert. A flash survey of her life confirmed this to be a common occurrence. Being ready, as far as discipline, was one thing; readiness for the life changes that had overtaken her and her friends was unattainable. She offered a silent prayer of thankfulness, and like her husband, allowed her training to focus her mind on task once again.

This Ulysses, sporting a much less than glamorous image, opened the dock door to receive the waiting teams of Shǒuhù Zhě.

"Greetings, Earthlings!", Loaf called out in his best fake alien voice. It was a bit uncanny. The thought of an alien would be a less impressive sight to behold than that of Sergeant Loaf. It could never compete with his aroma either.

"Howdy Meathead!" Louie shouted out as he and the others found their seats and strapped in for the ride, "Good thing we're not vegans. A protein pilot's the way to fly!" Groans filled the cabin from every occupant.

"How far away is it, Loaf?" Bob asked.

"We'll be there in a few minutes." Loaf responded as he engaged the drives to full thrust. The ship rocketed off the landing pad with a wide swing away from the embassy.

"Wouldn't want to chip that place again!" Loaf exclaimed as the crew behind him felt an intense rush of adrenaline, the G forces crushing their bodies opposite the trajectory of the ship.

"It's good to be with all of you again." Flip called out above the roar of the engines, "Maybe it's my instinctive need to be with my school."

"I can't say I've ever thought of being a fish Flip! But I'll swim with you any day." Louie yelled back then added sarcastically, "Just keep me away from the flashy lures. I know I'd be suckered". The bad jokes did little to stave off an unspoken thought of sacrifice lingering amongst this school of friends. They were for each other, freedom, individual responsibility, and honor. They loved their new homeworld and its purpose as a light to all who encountered it. They were happy to help protect their neighbors. Each was willing to lay down their lives for this cause. What they were most concerned with was losing each other. They had, as Flip had mentioned, become like a school. Not a mindless group held together by intimidation, fear, or control like the enemy's tactics. They were of one mind in purpose, vision, faith, and love. Now, as a group, they reminded themselves of their training, like Abner and Jenny, muting emotion, knowing the battle lay ahead.

The city of Kjett flashed below them as chemtrails of anti-DDM compound rained down to the surface from the ships overhead. Quandros was guilty of collaboration with The Collective. The Allies agreed that allowing The Yeasts to control the Quandrosite population was not only antithetical to victory but a merciless option. In an act of forbearance, they had decided against bombing the planet in favor of crop-dusting. The anti-DDM agent, now enriching the atmosphere, would provide relief within the hour, even in the smallest concentrations.

Reunion

The Ulysses roared above the outskirts of Kjett, climbing over the peaks of the Fjlett mountains on the outskirts of the city. Loaf called out to the crew,

"Hold on tight!" as he again hit full thrust beyond the highest peaks then passing over the high desert valley. A few more minutes elapsed as the Hydra's radar signature came into view on the instruments.

"Let's put er' down here..." Loaf spoke out loud to himself while eyeing a depression in the rocky landscape a mile from the enemy. The ship dropped out of the air with stealth to gently rest in what appeared to be an ancient crater. He surveyed the surroundings and pondered the metaphor of their impact upon this world and its implications. An uncanny feeling came to mind as he recalled the observations of Earth's past extinction event and the crater damage to its moon. It was a judgment upon that world. It appeared Earth might have been the focus but, Quandros was affected along with all of creation. Somehow, landing within this crater seemed to have a parallel impact to that of the past's judgment.

The teams of Shǒuhù Zhě began to disembark the Ulysses as ten more troop transports carrying ground forces from the various allied systems landed within the massive crater. A great representation of the Shǒuhù Zhě of Jook-Sing began to assemble. They included those of the New Seattle Junxio and the House of Swords. Unlike the camouflaged soldiers of the regular armed forces, their ranks attracted attention like gravity. The entire ensemble of soldiers and Shǒuhù Zhě were an emphatic statement of power, honor, and courage.

Jelly spoke through her comm to those related to the New Seattle Junxio,

"We are Shǒuhù Zhě! We have been prepared for this day by our Creator! I myself am the least of all. I am not a native of Jook-Sing. I am not the most powerful of this force. I am not the wisest. Hell, I'm not even fully human! I know these truths YET; I know our Creator has given me all I need for victory! He has prepared every one of you equally! We move together in Him against this evil before us! We will not fail! WE WILL NOT FAIL!

"The ground shook as the forces of Shǒuhù Zhě stomped the earth twice and loudly echoed her words,

"WE WILL NOT FAIL! WE WILL NOT FAIL!"

The allied soldiers nearby listening in were also emboldened by her words and the response of the Shǒuhù Zhě.

The roar of fighters overhead and defensive cannons emanating from the Hydra itself in the distance were deafening. Loaf called out, "Keep that distraction active, Pops! The exterminators are on their way!"

"Let's get this over with, kids! I'm getting thirsty for a pint!" Colonel Gleek responded. He continued to fly sorties above the enemy in attempts to weaken its defenses further. The Hydra's defensive shields began to deteriorate as a fighter under Colonel Gleek's command penetrated the aft defense making a direct hit to the main engines. The Hydra was now immobile. There was not an option to get out and push. The once frightening weapon of the enemy had become nothing more than a metallic hulk filled with hatred. The fighters continued to pummel the Hydra, one by one, taking out its cannons as the ground forces arrived within a quarter-mile of sight.

Inside the Hydra, the Monster spoke with his beloved. The two had become inseparable friends, feeding off of each other's hatred. Brain Jung did what any friend would do for the one he loved; he preserved it. Taking several test tubes, he gathered as many spores as possible and placed the tubes in a secure safe. Brian knew The Collective's time was short while stuffing the vessels into the specially prepared vault. Rage began to rise within the man as he closed the door on his comrade's future. The Collective spoke, "Brian, you of all humanity have been gracious to us. We will not forget your actions. If we prevail today, we will gladly share in the torment we will unleash on all who oppose us. You will devour the enemy in the face of its God! We honor you as a friend and bless all you do." The Yeasts were shaken to their core at the prospect of losing everything. It placed its future into the hands of Mr. Jung, its equal. Its remaining sentience was still present amongst the Monster, his twelve Tolkite mercenaries, the regular hosts of Tolkee, and the remaining Quandrosite forces aboard the Hydra. It prayed to itself in the hope of victory. The Collective was unsure for the first time of its future. It would not die quietly.

The Hydra's hatch opened, the gangplank extended as The Monster, along with the Twelve, raced down it toward their enemy. The remaining hosts flooded out onto the desert floor, with the Quandrosite host last to emerge. It was evident the front, and rear troops had hemmed in those in the middle, knowing them to be the least loyal if their master's hold loosened.

In the first row of the regular host, Major Liu Zhi rushed in formation as a unit with the others under The Collective's control. The fighters, flying low overhead, began crop dusting those emerging from the Hydra with the anti-DDM chem-trail. The effect was almost immediate.

On a microscopic level, the yeast's eukaryotic cells responded to the treatment with alarm. Time slowed to a crawl as each sentient yeast cell of The Collective worked individually within its own war for survival. They desired the awareness of life above life itself. The paradox of desire for self and what it perpetuated on those it sought to dominate was without remorse or empathy.

The chemical now within each host's bloodstream began to overwhelm the parasite within the blood of its victims. Each yeast cell watched as thousands of its family members lost their minds, becoming their primitive selves once again. It was a kind of death: a helpless, fallen, failure. The Collective was no more, apart from the collection present in the test tubes within the vault onboard the Hydra.

One hundred or so hosts standing outside of their ship paused for five minutes as the reversal of control within them took place. The Allied force sprang to life and charged toward the stunned host. The Monster and his warriors stormed the teams of Shǒuhù Zhě, led by Jelly,

Píng, Jenny, and Abner. The Quandrosites at the rear of the hosts abandoned the regular host of Tolkee as well and charged toward the allied ranks. The remaining hosts, looking bewildered after losing their overlord, were presented with a choice. They had before them three alternatives. One was simply to surrender. The second choice was moving forward in the spirit of "The Call." Many could be seen as clearly making a choice either way in the presence of a fellow former host making the opposite decision.

What ensued following these decisions played out as a third choice. A war within the ranks began out of what was once a uniform force. Tolkites loyal to "The Call" began killing their former brothers in arms. Those Tolkites realizing surrender meant death by those on every side chose instead to defend themselves and fight against a greater evil than themselves. They had decided at what appeared to be their final moments to surrender to The Creator and fight for freedom.

Once again, in his right mind, Mr. Liu Zhi began by blocking a sword blow by the Tolkite confronting him. After the next thrust by his adversary, Liu was struck by a welcomed realization. He was once again within The Light, alive once again. The oppressive darkness was gone. The act of defense to his personal safety seemed a light and momentary affliction. He was pleased to have the ability to engage his enemy physically while simultaneously inviting his adversary to turn from "The Call" back to The Light. Those adherents to "The Call" became more and more desperate as the violence intensified. One by one, they succumbed to failure as fatigue overwhelmed them. Almost as though under orders from an unseen force, they began to fall on their swords. Each would witness another from a distance and choose a similar end. When all had developed, one quarter remained of the one hundred and fifty former Tolkee hosts. The survivors spread out, joining the Allies against the Quandrosites.

In the Image of God

The half-burned Monster's eyes met those of the leading Shǒuhù Zhě before him. For a brief moment, he stopped dead as memory flooded his mind of what these people had taken from him. He had dreamt of this moment. The rage within him surged for the loss of his arm and the burns covering his body. His interaction with The Collective had been a solace after his last confrontation with these people. He was now keenly aware he was once again without the companionship of an equal. His wrath grew as the understanding of eminent isolation beyond this moment became apparent. Those before him became nothing more than objects of targeted rage.

Jenny stared back into the eyes of Brian "The Monster" Jung. She could not help but feel pity for him while reading him without the interference of The Collective. His history flashed before her with crushing tragedy. Jenny almost dropped her defenses. She was also able to see the series of choices made over this man's lifetime and of the rejection of mercy presented by The Creator. The Monster was all that was left. He had permanently seared his conscience against anything good. The inclinations of his heart were nothing more than continuous evil.

In the flash of time that these realizations took place, she was struck by something she saw deep within him. It was a disturbing sight to look into the eyes of someone made in the image of God and seeing only saturated indifference and hate. In this moment she could clearly see the concept fueled by deception that was accepted by many that equated our fallenness with God's character. Comfort consoled her knowing The Creator has no trace of our fallen nature though we are made in his image.

The twelve Tolkite mercenaries bolted out in front of The Monster before he could strike, engaging the ranks of Shǒuhù Zhě in a fury. At this point, it was apparent their numbers were falling on their own. The Tolkites continuously glanced behind them to see their army at war with itself. They steeled themselves, turning back toward the Allies and death.

The distance between opponents disappeared as swords, axes, and cudgels became a blur. The fury of Brian's men was countered with controlled reciprocal blocks by the Shǒuhù Zhě. By this time, it was difficult not to notice the scene taking place within the center of the Hydra's foot soldiers. Abner distracted by what appeared to be a war within their ranks, narrowly missed a fatal blow by his adversary. He managed to focus at the last moment stopping the blade inches from his neck. The weapon tore through his cloak and sliced open his flesh. The wound spanned the center of his chest to the shoulder. This surface wound burned across his torso, refocusing his attention to his opponent.

The scene became a distraction to all, and they separated momentarily to pause the fray. The Quandrosites were filling the ranks behind The Monster, and the Twelve as the hosts of Tolkee consumed themselves. At that moment, like a berserker, the Monster crashed through the twelve straight for Jelly. Slashing wildly at the blurred creature that was once stationary, his rage and frustration increased. While he was occupied, his men once again engaged the battle. The Monster stopped for a split second to regroup as Jelly's blade came down upon his head, removing an ear. She was visible once again, and his pain and loss, a token added to the hatred that consumed him. Like lightning, he slashed out as Jelly once again bounded acrobatically away from his blows. She stopped, looking down at her left forearm to see a deep gash beginning to bleed. He advanced toward her again as Layerie intervened, striking him at the left shoulder. The Monster turned with an earthmover's torque to cut Layerie's left leg off below the knee. He fell there as The Monster callously stepped on his severed leg in his way, breaking its bones.

"NOOOOOOO!" Jelly cried out in anger while running at The Monster as blood poured from her wound. She flew through the air too fast for him to avoid the second slashing blow that removed his remaining ear. The sounds all around him became a muted, distorted, swirling abstraction. It was so distracting; he lost all sense of position. Looking behind himself, he saw Jelly fall to the ground beside Layerie. He turned his attention toward Abner, who began his attack. The anamorphic sounds continued to plague him as he forced his hatred to bloom. Blocking Abner's blade with a circular motion, he thrust his short sword into his attacker's chest. Abner stumbled backward, grasping at the hole in his breast, then, remembering his emergency kit, fell weakly to the ground. Mr. Jung turned his attention once again to the ranks of Tolkee host behind him to see most of them fallen, some actively fighting each other or the Quandrosite guard. It was too confusing. He chose to ignore his fate and turned back toward the front with wrath. He was consumed within an almost psychedelic psychopathic state of evil. The rage within could not be contained as his body shook with tremors while he roared at the ranks of Shǒuhù Zhě before him.

Jenny, the closest to him, thrust against one of the Tolkites incapacitating him, turned toward Brian with pity. She read him with trepidation, sensing every neuron's stored bit of memory within a flash of time. His eyes locked onto her as he somehow knew she was within his thoughts. A contrast of hope and hatred developed within his eyes and the thoughts Jenny read within him. Like an oppressive hand that enveloped him and shown in his eyes, the light within him was extinguished by darkness. It became overwhelming. She could not remain and let go of his mind. A representative of distilled evil was now before her.

She pondered once again, the blasphemy of evil using a vessel made in the image of The Creator. It was a tragic, pitiful sight that caused shivers to run up her spine. She steeled herself, turning toward her training once again. The training was what would save her life and those dear to her.

Quandrosite artillery projectiles began falling all around them. This distraction was what the twelve needed. They once again saved their leader, this time against his will. A sedative was required. The Monster would not have retreated willingly. The Shǒuhù Zhě and Quandrosite hosts scattered beneath the barrage raining down from above. Brian Jung felt a sting in his neck. His men dragged him back to The Hydra's shuttle.

Jenny searched out Abner. She came upon him just before he passed out after using a void filler to contain his wound. She stroked his head and kissed him gently as the Allied medic ships arrived. The medics began descending upon the battlefield. Two medics scanned him for vitals,

"He's gonna be okay, Shifu. Looks like he used the filler in time. We need to get him outta here, though. He has lost a lot of blood. We'll keep you informed, ma'am." He and his fellow medic then quickly carried him to the transporter. Now hopeful, Jenny watched as Jelly, Layerie, and remaining Shǒuhù Zhě survivors were taken away along with their wounded opponents.

Symbolically, it appeared that one of the Hydra's heads had been cut off as one of its shuttles detached and rocketed away. The Collective seemed to have lost one of its own as well. Like the ancient Greek legend, this beast's fight was not over.

Tag Team

Over time, Danielle had learned how to separate her thoughts from that of the SNAM. She could reason like a human while simultaneously receiving the assistance of this AI. It was an interface few could understand. She was astonished at how this technology had pierced through the time-space continuum beyond mere observance.

After Marcus explained the best ways to pass through the portals, the SNAM took over once again. She watched Marcus jump headfirst into the portal, his body disappearing as it entered the void. Danielle walked with mixed feelings of excitement and fear to the edge of the portal. She wanted to test the waters with her toe but instead made a perfect jump headlong through. At the next level below, Marcus was ready to catch her, knowing the trial and error he had endured. There was no need as SNAM had calculated everything necessary. It was like observing a gold medal Olympian land at the edge of the next portal. Danielle regained her composure while looking at Marcus.

"That was a rush!"

"I wish I had it down like you. I'm still doing this while holding my breath!" Marcus replied.

Danielle stopped as SNAM's calculations whirred.

"Hold on... SNAM's checking this level."

"Okay, I'm in no hurry, just glad we have some kind of direction."

"Nope, not this one either. SNAM says six more levels might be closer to where we need to be. Whadda you think?"

"Well, you know how my track record's been. Let's give it a shot, can't hurt."

Marcus began his consecutive jumps, resting after each, just long enough to regain his composure. He made sure Danielle had passed through each level after him. The final jump was completed as he waited for Danielle's entry. She once again stuck her landing to Marcus' amazement and not without a touch of envy.

"Well, what does SNAM have to say now?" Marcus inquired.

"SNAM says she was here last. She could be anywhere, though. We've found her time. We just need to find her space."

The three companions- Danielle, Marcus, and SNAM, had been within this realm for over a week now. They were oblivious to the war taking place on Quandros; otherwise, they would have been alongside their comrades. Nevertheless, this was a crusade with equal implications. Time was starting to become an abstract state of mind as the three wandered its corridors.

The Creator and Christy continued their conversation, for lack of a better term: every day- as time was irrelevant. She was well aware of being outside of time and space in a place only accessible by The Creator. It was the space between the Christy shaped holes. While in the arms of her Savior, she knew even the quantum portals couldn't contain Him. They had been in and out of time and space. Within His domain- eternity, in and outside of his creation.

Understanding this, The Creator mentioned Christy's need to reenter the quantum realm. He explained how her friends were searching for her and how others were affected by the quantum weapon. She was reassured they would never be parted in His Spirit. Christy was hesitant to leave Him. She decided to take comfort in knowing it wasn't her time to continue this walk throughout eternity. The Creator stopped within thequantum step below the chosen point of time and space. With a presence, only He could have, smiled and touched her cheek. She knew this was His goodbye for now. She grasped by faith He would return.

At that moment, Marcus dropped through the portal above her. Once again, hitting his head on her outlined shape as he did. He lay there on the ground before her for a second as his eyes cleared. Christy came into view as she stood smiling above him.

"Glad you could drop in, Marc!" she said with an otherworldly, contented smile that equally comforted and scared him. He sat up, smiled saying,

"I found you! I've been so worried. We have a lot to talk about, but, first, we need to get you back home!"

"Marc, it's been amazing, but I'm ready to go home with you." Christy stepped back with amusement as Danielle dropped from the portal above to the ground next to Marcus sitting by the portal.

"We found you, Stacy! I knew we would!" Danielle beamed with joy, embracing her friend. Christy decided it best to allow them to believe that they had found her. She smiled in her heart toward The Eternal as she helped Marcus to his feet. The three companions began their ascent to the present. Christy was struck with the concept of time. After her experiences, it was almost humorous.

The return home was within view now. Marcus reached up to the rim of the portal above after Christy and Danielle had passed through it. He stopped, pulling his hand back momentarily. There was an overwhelming feeling of thankfulness that overpowered him. He began to weep with joy and spoke out loud to The Creator, "I can count on you. You know me. Thank you." Marcus wiped his eyes and once again grabbed hold of the portal's rim and pulled himself up.

All around them, New Seattle bustled with activity. The three had no idea the war was raging on Quandros. There was an electric feel in the air, charged with equal measures of fear and hope. Danielle or rather SNAM spoke first,

"These are the images I am experiencing..." immediately, SNAM projected the experiences to Danielle of the developments associated with the Hydra and its occupants upon Quandros. SNAM spoke again. Danielle, it may be advantageous for your narration of these events for your friends. I am keenly aware of my failings associated with human interactions."

Danielle explained all that had occurred according to SNAM's precognitions. As difficult as it was for Marcus to leave Christy, he knew he must be involved with keeping her

and the free worlds alive. The three walked
Christy to her home and ran to The House of
Swords.

Before her experiences, Christy would have
panicked. Worry would have gained a
prominent place in every thought until Marcus'
return. Things were much different now. She
was changed from within her spirit. There was
a deep peace within her soul, the lingering
Spirit of The One outside of time and space.
She had walked with Him. It was different
from reading scripture or listening to accounts
of other's experiences with the supernatural.
Yes, there was an element of the metaphysical,
but this was not merely a feeling, emotion, or
even a miraculous event she had encountered.
Christy had become familiarized with The
Divine. She had touched Him, spoken with
Him, walked with Him. He had confirmed
scripture to her and none of her experiences or
conversation with Him conflicted with the
written word. Everything now made sense.

She did her best to allow humility to guide her
interactions with those who had no idea why
she had changed.

Ground Beef?

The Allies were in the process of landing
and infiltrating every known Quandrosite
political, military, and intelligence site on the
planet. The troop transports landed near the
major cities of Kjett, Leifljite, Quanyv, and
every populated province on the surface.
Surface to air defenses and Quandrosite
fighters could not stave off the overwhelming
numbers of the Allied fleet. The anti-DDM
treatments had rendered The Collective's
physical influence on Quandros null.
Unfortunately, the Collective's lingering
influence over the cult of "The Call" had
grown within the ranks of the military. The
contrasting fear and despair of the invasion
overtook the general population. Quandrosite
culture had begun to be turned upside down
only twenty-four hours after the attack began.
Large divisions of the populous called for
surrender, betraying the confidence of the
military. The polarization within the society
caused a slow collapse. Radical adherents to
The Call within the military began acts of

domestic terrorism, adding to the strife of this world. The seeds were sown toward hatred, greed, narcissism, and political superiority began to ripen with fruition. The Collective had given a final directive before its isolation to those within The Call. It urged them toward extremism, pushing them to hatred against the moderates of their world. The Quandrosite society, rooted in self, quickly imploded. It became an obvious example of judgment against a culture built on the key pillars of evil. Future history would prove the civil war that ensued within an already crushing invasion from without, depleted the legacy of the Quandrosite people to a scattered remnant.

Colonel Gleek's time was occupied with defending the transport ships alongside his squadron of Commonwealth fighters. He was confused as to why there had not been more significant resistance from the surface. He watched a formation of Quandrosite GWTs turn away from engagement with his squadron to dive-bomb and fire upon its own homeland.

This is insanity! What is wrong with them? Well, I guess it makes our job easier... He pondered while escorting another transport toward the surface near Kjett's capitol building.

"Can you believe this? I knew these people were different, but this is insane." He said through his comm to Loaf. "To think the Morfarians have been putting up with neighbors like these for a millennium!"

"It really seems like a dream, doesn't it! Marcus Filet is the only Quandrosite I've known personally. He was a real piece of work before his change. I would think this would be tough for him to witness. I don't care how screwed up family is. Seeing it fall apart like this would be heartbreaking."

"You know, Loaf, you've got a lot of wisdom for a meatloaf."

"Thanks, Pops! Must be in the genes. Watch your six!" Colonel Gleek evasively rolled and looped in the opposite direction, narrowly avoiding another lone GWT on a collision course. The enemy fighter mindlessly continued its trajectory, now in full thrust into the city's highest tower building. The ship vaporized in a fireball impacting and destroying the top three floors.

"I don't know which is worse, the danger of being in this or watching them kill themselves!" Colonel Geek exclaimed.

"All I can say is, let's get this done quick!" Loaf replied as his perspiration filled the Ulysses' cockpit with a savory aroma.

The colonel made it to their targeted site and waited for the soldiers to disembark the transport. Loaf also landed and waited patiently for his troops to hit the ground. The last warrior left the ship and slapped its hull twice as an "all clear" signal to Loaf. Both he in the Ulysses and the troop transport lifted off the surface to head back to the retrieval site.

Ramar looked to the south toward the city and a known artillery battery installation as the cannons began to fill the sky with projectiles.

"Let's get the hell outta' here, Loaf!"

"I'm on it, just one sec......"

It was too late as the Ulysses was struck in the aft section of the ship. The main engine was obliterated, leaving only the side thrusters for propulsion. Loaf worked hard at correcting a severe rotation of the ship's longitudinal axis. The ship spun in the air like a slow propeller as Loaf pulled its nose up to counteract the rotation. For fifteen seconds, Ramar could do nothing but watch his newly found offspring fight for his life. As the colonel observed, he couldn't help but comment on the procedure within himself. Loaf had done everything with perfect timing in keeping with Ramar's thought. It was as though he was piloting remotely. Loaf corrected the spin and attempted to pull the ship out of a nosedive with an eighth of the power previously available. The Ulysses leveled off and dropped parallel to the ground for a belly landing. The force began to tear the ship apart from the underside upward. A quarter-mile after impact, it came to rest in a cornfield.

Ramar snapped out his stunned state and rocketed toward the now immobile Ulysses. The rear of the ship erupted in flame and heavy black smoke as he arrived at the scene. Ramar instinctively grabbed his respirator and emergency kit. He ran to the wreck, first tossing out a fire block canister and two halon grenades. He watched to make sure everything was deployed correctly. As the projectiles were airborne, he couldn't help but worry, knowing he hadn't checked the expiration date on the kit lately. To his relief, the halon grenades and fire block detonated perfectly. He turned quickly toward the cockpit emergency access port. Arriving underneath the nose of the ship, he could hear pounding upon the hatch. The colonel pulled a crowbar from his kit and began to pry open the door. One more impact was heard before the door violently slapped free against the hull. Loaf shimmied through the opening to the ground below. Relived, Ramar exclaimed,

"That was close! You did an excellent job, Son. I'm kinda proud of Y'all."

"I admit that was the scariest thing I've ever done. I thought for sure that was it!"

"Well, I do like the lightly burnt ends of a meatloaf but, I'm glad you're okay!"

"I'm not sure how to respond to that one Pops."

"I'll let ya'll think about it. Meantime we better get outta here. Come on!"

The two sprinted back to the colonel's fighter as Quandrosite bombers began pummeling the landscape a mile northwest of them. Once within the safety of the ship and its shield generator, Ramar lifted heavenward as they both viewed the crash site. Loaf couldn't help but become emotional viewing the crippled remains of his youth abandoned to Quandrosite soil. Time stood still as the memories played out in his mind. Abruptly, a blinding white flash had overpowered his view of the Ulysses. The flash was replaced with fire and smoke that rose upward. The Ulysses was replaced by no more than random deformed chunks of metal and debris nearby the cratered blast zone. Loaf, shocked by the sudden loss of the second Ulysses, treasured its memory within as he clutched its ignition keys.

Two Perspectives of Prey

Ramar transported Loaf to rejoin the Shǒuhù Zhě outside the small town of Ekte on the outskirts of Kjett. News of the Ulysses hit hard for all momentarily then was stored for later as each focused on their objectives. Intel had directed them to this village as a possible location for The Twelve. The former Commonwealth Shǒuhù Zhě joined another squadron of the House of Swords to root out the enemy. The predators were now the prey. Both divisions began to move like the wind through the town. Each home encountered held cowering residents. Those who had previously experienced the twelve held an unmistakable terror in their eyes. As each Shǒuhù Zhě reported their findings, the pattern emerged, pointing them toward the northeastern boundary of the town.

The teams began to move toward the Twelve, finding a breadcrumb trail of Quandrosite body parts as they neared the target. Marcus led his team of five like fire freshly oxygenated. Each dismemberment he passed in route fueled his need to extinguish the evil responsible. The team followed behind, consisting of Danielle, Louie, Flip, Rob, and Angie. They coursed through the maze of the town like spirit undeterred. Ahead of them lay a mountain cave. On either side of the path leading toward its entrance lay heads, limbs, and entrails. The discarded remnants of the twelve's meal- an unholy last supper.

At this time, the Monster recovered from the drug-induced abduction by his companions. He and five of the twelve were now awaiting their enemy within a house a quarter-mile from the cave. He and these Tolkites had chosen to break off to hide in ambush. The six additional elite men were within the cave as an attempt to draw their enemies within. The twelfth Tolkite had fallen by the hand of the Acorn. This revelation added fuel to Brian's need for revenge. He allowed a mixture of hatred and fury to flow within himself while in a euphoric state of mind.

Jenny's team arrived last at the cave site. The group consisted of Rob, Maude, Loaf, and Cedric. Overhead, a squadron of Quandrosite fighters began to pummel the ground with munitions while simultaneously fighting off Allied soldiers. One by one, after being hit, they aimed their disabled GWTs toward the battle scene. The Shǒuhù Zhě moved like pendulums, undeterred, avoiding the incoming, all attention on the mouth of the cave.

First to arrive, Marcus and his team entered the cave entrance to find it leading down into the roots of the mountain. All but Jenny's comrades followed Marcus into the subterranean karst complex. Over the following thirty minutes, the overhead battle died out as the majority of the GWTs lay within a mile radius. Minutes became hours as Jenny and her team waited outside the cave for signs of activity.

"I can't see us waiting outside any longer," Jenny said as the sunlight began to dwindle. "We should move below ground."

The team agreed as they entered the mouth of the cave. Each member switched on their headlamps, causing the cave's interior to come alive out of the shrouded darkness. The majestic stalactites and stalagmites now visible gave this underworld a similar feel to that of a cathedral. The topography created multiple patterns of possible paths ahead. They decided to allow Cedric's nose to lead the way toward the enemy. The group followed the eflume to the mouth of a tunnel branching from the cave's main room. They wandered deeper into the depths, sometimes squeezing through tight holes in the fallen rock. Jenny, always following from behind, assisted those ahead past the obstructions. The enemy was rewarded by drawing all teams into the depths of the underworld. The hours lingered as each member of the Shǒuhù Zhě forces struggled to focus on the Truth. It was as though the unseen forces of darkness were raging all around them for supremacy. The physical absence of Light equaled the oppressive reality around them. Marcus, sensing the foreboding dominance around him that vied for his attention, recounted the Truth to himself as he prayed to The Creator. He struggled to press through, focusing on The Spirit of Light. The experience around him attempted to dull his senses and drive his heart to despair. A shimmer of hope glowed within him; the darkness was unable to extinguish its ever-growing flame. He opened his commlink to the others,

"There's more than physical darkness here, folks. Don't lose focus. Remember your training. Our Light is not only physical. Look to The Creator, know He is with us. He said He has bonded to our spirits. It doesn't matter if you can't feel that- IT'S TRUE!" As Marcus spoke, the darkness began to lose its power to subjugate. It was obvious to all involved there had been a powerful change in their once missing shifu. The trials experienced in his search for Christy had combined into a profound asset to the man's ability to trust in providence. He was keenly aware of every one of their needs being met by The Eternal One.

The Shǒuhù Zhě revived as a unit. A peace rekindled within each warrior. All at once, the Tolkites attacked within the narrow subterranean crevasse from ledges twenty feet above on either side. Rocks rained down on the center of the column of Shǒuhù Zhě, causing them to divide. Half moved deeper into the caves. The others backed away from the assault. As they did, those closest to the center began to scale the cave walls, with stealth, toward the insurgents above.

Now leading her team outward to regroup, Jenny began to sense a presence similar to the darkness they all had experienced earlier. The distinction in this experience was that it was emanating from a singular being. It was filled to overflowing with the same malevolence. She knew what lay ahead of her around the corner in the darkness. Motioning her team and those behind them to hold their ground, she switched off her headlamps. Jenny put all of her focus on The Spirit of The Creator and began to see through the darkness. With sword drawn, she ran in power toward the enemy then, up the wall on her left. She made a spinning strike while rebounding toward the opposite wall downward. The hunter then became prey. The Monster grasped at his freshly wounded scalp. Blood obscured his eyes as his forehead and hairline became loose. His face drooped, further disfiguring his visage to match the evil within himself. Mr. Jung's groans gradually turned to a rage-filled bellow as he slashed wildly at his unseen enemy.

Once again, his defenders engaged as Jenny's team joined the battle. Jenny, became aware she was within a place she hadn't known before. She reasoned The Creator had allowed all of her previous experience to coalesce within her for this moment in time. She knew He was directing everything within her. She moved throughout the cave unhindered, taking down every opponent she engaged. While attempting to assist, her team stepped back, stunned as they watched what they knew was a supernatural display. Brian Jung stood his ground with a brooding animus at the sight of every Tolkite dead at his feet.

Commitment

Brian "The Monster" Jung recommitted his heart to bitterness, hatred, and revenge. He began to allow the memory of his conversations with The Collective to permeate his being. Once a primitive Quandrosite cult, the Call was perfected by the evil present in the mind of The Collective. A love for his friend, now hidden away physically, was allowed full reign within himself. Mr. Jung once thought he was above the need of The Call, welcomed its blind adherence to evil. A spiritual power overtook him as he turned his eyes from his fallen ranks toward Jenny. The two engaged with fury.

The remaining Tolkites in the center of the cave began to move outward toward the divided forces of Shǒuhù Zhě. Jenny's team had no choice but to engage those at their rear flank while leaving Jenny to defend herself. The Monster roared as he lashed out at what appeared to be a streak of blinding white light before him. Unable to contact his foe, he fumed with frustration. Jenny, with unearthly agility, moved around his weapon as though time was abated.

A company of Quandrosite adherents to The Call began to fill the cave complex from unseen entrances above. They weaved downward from the ledges to assist the remaining Tolkites. The Shǒuhù Zhě engaged the newcomers while attempting to neutralize the remaining Tolkites. Each was overwhelmed while trying to contain the chaotic situation as the darkness increased below ground. It became apparent the spiritual darkness was manifesting in the physical as each new Quandrosite entered the cave complex. All began to pray and trust The Eternal One above the circumstance playing out before them.

Jenny and The Monster were left to themselves in what appeared to both as a cosmic battle. Using brute force, Mr. Jung joined to an unseen power within the darkness stabbed toward the Shǒuhù Zhě before him. Jenny had somehow tapped into energy she knew could only be described as a holy fury. She had become a tool in the hands of The Creator. Jenny had surrendered herself to His will, and there was no hatred of her enemy involved. She was nothing more than a weapon of judgment as her sword pierced The Monster's heart. She felt The Creator's heart break at this loss. The experience validated her own feelings of past experiences in these situations. This knowledge, now in unison with the Spirit of The Creator, was overwhelming.

Brian Jung, the complete being fell. Viewed outside of time from The Creator's perspective, he appeared from infancy to the moment of death. His blood poured from his chest, a blood unable to cover the sins of a being who refused to turn from evil. He had been given the fullness of time to receive forgiveness by a blood shed from the one and only Savior. The Creator took no pleasure in The Monster's death. His body went limp in the darkness as the life drained from him. The darkness callously received him to itself, aware it too would be judged at a future time. It treasured another foolish pawn until its own appointed time of judgment.

Jenny stopped to grieve over her foe as he exhaled his last breath. She noted a look of terror in his eyes after switching on her headlamp as it cut through the darkness. She couldn't help but feel a deep sense of pity for him after having tapped into his mind many times. In their encounters, knowing his story, it was impossible not to wish things had been different for him. Jenny could linger no longer and turned to rejoin the battle deeper within the karst world around her.

Unaware of Brain's fall, three of the remaining Tolkites left the battle scene according to Their lord's direction. These three tore themselves away from the fray and ascended to the surface as the last Quandrosites entered. Once beyond the focus of battle, they made their way back to the Hydra. The ten-mile hike brought them to the ship as the sun began to set. The Hydra lay before them, a wreck bereft of its former dread. Keith Glemick, Jason Royce, and Gene Fry- The Three. The Three were Brian Jung's most loyal men. They had been his primary protectors in days past. They had coordinated his rescue on more than one occasion. They knew his limitations and were his greatest assets. The Three had failed to protect their lord. They would soon learn this bitter truth, yet, at this time, they were concerned with nothing but obeying his last words. His directive was given prior to engagement with the Shǒuhù Zhě, "If our plan fails, the three of you must retrieve The Collective at any cost!" The Three entered the ship intent on conserving this force necessary for their continued survival.

Jenny rejoined her comrades deeper within the cave system. She looked to her left to see Cedric rushing through a group of Quandrosite troops. These rivals seemed to possess a determined spirit, unlike many encountered previously. There was division amongst the Quandrosite military. Jenny had once thought they had turned as a whole against the population of the planet in rebellion. These men were of a different cut from those participating in Quandros' civil war. Though determined, they were no match for the eflume. Cedric's charge had left four men on the ground, the others he had cast into the nearest walls.

All around her, Shǒuhù Zhě were engaged with the remaining Quandrosites. She began to take an inventory of the remaining Tolkites. Marcus was paired with one, Louie battled another roughly thirty feet away. Danielle was defending herself as a third resident of the dead moon attacked. Jenny concluded the remaining three were hidden or, worse yet, in retreat. Just then, she heard the distinct sound of a Quandrosite blade pass over her head as she unconsciously ducked away from its path.

Without thinking, Jenny once again was moved as an instrument of judgment. She became a blinding white flash, an inner light similar yet more potent than the glow present within her during her change in the landfill. The underground world was instantly illuminated as Jenny's form flashed amongst those who attempted to resist. The sight became a powerful distraction to all. The Shǒuhù Zhě took advantage of the situation

and dispatched their adversaries. The battle
ended in the last flash of the streaking Shǒuhù
Zhě as she cut down the last remaining foe.
The battle was over. Those who had
committed to their cause had chosen their
outcome. Many Shǒuhù Zhě had given their
lives for the freedom of others. Brian Jung and
nine of his Tolkites had shed their blood for
selfishness and rage. Many Quandrosites had
joined them in this foolishness. The contrast
was evident upon the faces of the dead. The
forces of evil had been abated in the darkness
today. Jenny gathered her comrades to inform
them of the three remaining Tolkites.

"Anyone have any ideas?" Jenny called out,
eager to pursue the enemy.

"They could be anywhere," Flip warned.

"I just had one of those visions, Jenny!",
Danielle yelled out.

"Go on!" she responded.

"I saw the Hydra again. It looked different,
though."

"Well, that's good enough for me, let's go!"
Cedric roared.

The group arrived in a transport ten
minutes later at the site of the fallen ship. It
had indeed changed. Another "head" was
missing, and they were aware its second
shuttle had detached. Somewhat discouraged,
they boarded the ship for any clues to the
Tolkite's destination. The fruitless search

ended as the group allowed the truth to sink in. Their efforts this day had been rewarded, yet the fight would continue.

Reprieve

The Hydra lay lifeless upon the plains within twenty miles of Kjett. The Allies called in a salvage crew to remove all tech and weaponry. This instrument of terror now bereft of spirit seemed a mere monument to the evil it once possessed. The sight of the incapacitated ship gave Marcus a measure of relief. The knowledge of the three missing Tolkites was a deep concern to him and his fellow Shǒuhù Zhě. For now, he was content with the damage done to the enemy's cause. The Quandrosite civil war continued even after the last Allied ship departed its airspace. Quandros had been a hotspot for societal unrest from its antiquity. This civilization rejected The Creator and his plan of redemption. Without His intervention, it would continue its strife.

The wounded were sent to various hospitals on Jook-Sing as the war began to fade. Abner, Jelly, and Layerie were brought to New Seattle. Layerie, who sustained the most significant injuries, was stable in the ICU with a new robotic prosthetic leg. Jelly had blacked out from her wounds, was stitched up, given blood, and at Layerie's bedside. Abner had also lost consciousness due to blood loss was fortunate to have stopped most of his bleeding beforehand. A punctured lung and chest injury mended; he lay in the bed opposite Layerie heavily sedated. Jenny rushed to his side upon arrival and waited for his awakening.

Early in the following week, the three wounded comrades revived within hours of each other to the relief of their friends. Layerie and Jelly were content to have the tragedy forced upon them to bring out their true feelings for one another. They spent much of the first day of recovery speaking from their respective hospital beds. In retrospect, they agreed this newly kindled romance was a critical factor in their recoveries' speed.

Jenny tapped into Abner's subconscious mind while deep in his comatose state from when she came to his bedside. A mere observer, she was once again unable to do anything to help her husband while his body and mind healed. She took comfort in witnessing this dream state, knowing his mind was alive. There was a piece of knowledge within her that this was yet another realm within the hand of The Eternal One. The Healer was at work in ways Jenny couldn't comprehend. She knew one fact only, a power was at work that emanated from the completed work done on a Roman death cross in the first century AD in Jerusalem, Earth. The Creator had walked this land as a man only to die for all of His creation. This death not only paid the debt of sins for all but was the source of all healing. The Eternal One, outside of His creation's time and space, was able to spend His wealth wherever he pleased. Jenny observed what she was able to comprehend with pure fascination.

Abner's eyes cleared along with his thoughts as Jenny held his hand.

"Hi," he said weakly with eyes focused on hers while attempting a smile, "how long have I been out?" Jenny gripped his hand tightly, responding,

"It's been about a week Abe. You've been pretty heavily sedated. The sword missed your heart but punctured a lung. The doctors say you're healing up well. I've been with you since Quandros ended."

"So, what happened? I just remember falling after their leader…The Monster, was it? Stabbed me. You don't know how helpless I felt before I blacked out. I thought that was it."

Jenny looked into his eyes and responded,

"I'm so glad the darkness didn't win Abe. The Eternal had His hand on us. We lost many good friends; they are with Him now. He struck down all but three Tolkites. The Monster is dead, and most of those from the Hydra. We don't know if The Collective is still active or not but, most of its teeth are gone now."

"That's a relief. Quandros?"

"Still in their civil war. The Allies pulled out. I can't see anything we do ending that."

"We'll need to keep tabs on the Morfarians."

"At least that system has a place of sanctuary for the ones seeking peace," Abner weakly responded as he slipped back to sleep.

Thankful for her husband's recovery, Jenny welcomed Píng, Loaf, Marcus, and Christy as they entered the room.

"He's just fallen back asleep along with those two." She pointed toward Jelly and Layerie. "this'll be a good time to get some lunch. He's doing great!" The five left the hospital in search of dim sum in the nearby row of restaurants.

They wandered into the first Cantonese establishment down the street. There behind the front desk, a familiar face greeted them with an equally recognizable voice.

"Dudes! I was hoping I'd scope you guys one day. This is totally awesome man. I'm psyched!" Enfreck Fren exclaimed as they entered the restaurant.

"En? Is that you?" Jenny practically shouted while knowing his appearance unmatched with memory was irrelevant. "You've changed! What are you doing here?" Enfreck's now long hair matching his persona no longer a distraction as he replied, "Jen, yeah, it's me, Dude! All of us were given a choice a few years ago. The off-boundary laws are like gone, man! I've been wanting to come here for like, forever, man. Got here last week after my visa was approved."

"I didn't realize The Commonwealth is free now! So, a restaurant? Kinda different from facilities?"

"Yeah, man. I think your gig's not so wrenchy either, Dude! You're like some kinda master warrior chick or something now, right? Dude, that's righteous!" Jenny chuckled to herself, seeing Enfreck.

He walked them to their table and sat down with them in the nearly empty dining hall as Jenny introduced him to the others.

"So, like it's pretty dead now, I'll take a break with you guys, K." He stood up awkwardly with memory, "I guess I need to get you some drinks first." He returned with five rice beers and sat down once again while sipping tea. "So like, how've you been? How's Abe?" distractedly, he looked over at Loaf, saying, "Not to be a jerk or anything, Man, but, you my friend are a trip! But, Dude, you smell delicious!" Loaf laughed and said, "En, I'm a Meatloaf. Don't ask me to explain but, thanks, I'll take the compliment!"

Conclusions

Now that Danielle, Christy, and Marcus were safely back on Jook-Sing and within their correct quantum present, the next step began to take place. A machine engineered by Professor Timothy Stanley, Cedric, and Danielle was brought to the Christy-shaped quantum portal, now covered with steel plating. The plates were removed as those present viewed the abyss with wonder and fear. A structure was placed above it, along with a rocket pointing downward.

Though able to empathize with those around her, Christy viewed the abyss of her likeness with an inward chuckle. Nothing could separate her from the security found in The Eternal One. She was able to view the sight before her with the memory of her experience with Him. In contrast to this, she could see the fascination of its form through the eyes of those around her. This visible example of endlessness was awe-inspiring. True eternity with The Creator made it pale in comparison. Backing away from the portal, she smiled at Marcus with the otherworldly smile he was becoming accustomed to.

Jenny and Marcus finalized all calculations for the machine. They decided to call this drone designed to close the time torn portals "The Zipper" to lighten the situation. Theoretically, these unmanned crafts fitted with reverse-engineered KP pulse modulators would be flown through each portal, dotting ten points on the surface of Jook-Sing. The weapon's polarity was inversed to close the quantum holes as it rocketed through the apertures.

The controls were set up to mimic two average KSP navigation interfaces. Jenny and Marcus took their places at respective helms and began their ballet of keyboard inputs, wheel turns, button hits, and joystick manipulations. The Quandrosite and the human who gleaned his skills danced inwardly with lightning-fast intellect and outwardly with agility on the controls as the colossal list of variables were input to the drone. These actions would need to be repeated for the next nine portals cut into the skin of New Seattle.

The dance concluded as each participant released their controls simultaneously in perfect sync. They stopped and looked at each other with concerned yet, hopeful expectations. Together without warning to the others, they hit the execute buttons on each control panel as the four-foot rocket came to life. The missile's tail cone emitted its nuclear-fueled exhaust flame as the launch gantry released its payload downward. The missile was immediately obscured by freshly closed ground after dropping past the portal. They left the rest to faith, knowing after the first portal breach had been closed, this and the others would be impossible to verify for success.

The next six months passed as a sense of normalcy returned. The authorities of Jook-Sing made sure to schedule regular anti-DDM chem-trail flyovers of Tolkee. There was no sense in gambling with the dark moon. It became apparent the hands-off approach of dealing with the penal colony had been a failure. A correctional force was set up to make regular observations of the inhabitants of the prison moon. It was difficult to imagine anything reoccurring on the scale of the Hydra's manufacturing without The Collective's influence. They had been short-sighted in the past; the hope was to prevent another failure.

The House of Swords recognized Liu Zhi for his efforts to defeat the enemy in the battle on Quandros. His life sentence was shortened to fifteen years on Tolkee for the bravery he had displayed. There was a change in the man's character. Even the knowledge of a return to Tolkee wasn't enough to darken his heart. He now knew the contrast between light and darkness and was determined to seek The Light for the rest of his days.

It was decided that Marcus would return to the junxio as shifu. Jelly was relieved Marcus had returned to what she and the others agreed was his calling. His presence enhanced the mood at the junxio. He and his new bride Christy were somewhat of a mystery to all. She, having endured a rupture through time and space, he the one who pursued her against all logic. Christy had joined the junxio as well and took up residency as a teacher. She was instrumental in equipping the students in the profound aspects of their faith in the One True Creator. Few were able to rival her faith as she had walked with God. Her humility in welcoming all to His richness was rooted in the knowledge of His presence verified by scripture. After walking with an omnipotent, equally humble being, there was no room for her self-aggrandizement. The couple became legendary and responsible for not only enhancing the junxio but Jook-Sing as a whole. It was evident The Creator had used the adversity of The Collective to draw the masses to a greater good.

A week after the time zippers had been launched, all were united at their favorite pub. Poontrip was served by Nomar Eleeskee, the much-loved E-Tollian whose grunts, clicks, shrieks, and sighs could be heard above the crowd's din and his translations. Many toasts were made as the assembly was joined in thankfulness to The Creator for His hand in their lives.

Ambassador Doncless made his way to a nearby microphone to address the group. He then tuned his translator before speaking, "I would like to say a few words if I may...." the crowd's noise settled to a low hum as he continued, "The events that played out in this last year, culminating upon Quandros, have shattered many of my own conceptions. I have served E-Toll and Quandros for decades. I justified many of my own questionable decisions as being for the good of both parties. I wasn't stretching the truth. I have just come to realize some of my dealings were self-serving. This is why I have decided to resign from my ambassadorship. When I looked into the eyes of Shifu Jelly, my rescuer, I knew what was truly important in life, life itself. I want to toast to the brave Shǒuhù Zhě who risked all to save me. In honesty, I'm not sure why I was saved. Nonetheless, I have made arrangements with the government of E-Toll to present a gift to Jelly and her companions. Please gather around, folks."

Jelly, Peanut, Jenny, Abner, Layerie, Loaf, Flip, Maude, Angie, Claus, Rob, Bob, Marcus, Basir, Claus, and Louie stepped forward.

"On behalf of the people of E-Toll and with my deepest appreciation, I would like to present the starship, the Ulysses, as a token of thanks to this band of friends." Doncless paused, smiled, and winked at them before stating, "May the pleasure of its use exceed your first encounter!" The joined friends stood dazed as the meaning of his words began to sink in. The Ulysses, no mere trinket of a reward, was theirs. A dream realized. They were overwhelmed and equally humbled. Jelly reluctantly reached out to receive keys and paperwork from their E-Tollian benefactor while straining against her legs of rubber.

Nomar Eleeskee, with excitement, called out,

"This calls for another round! Don't forget your enzyme pills, or all of us'll be sorry!"

Xytist Doncless warmly embraced Jelly and her friends before floating away upon his hovercart to the door where a transport waited outside to return him home to his beloved home on E-Toll. His heart full, he disregarded the greater G-load of Jook-Sing on his way outside. The E-Tollian's grunts, clicks, shrieks, and sighs faded as he departed.

List of Characters

of The Landfill Collective

*Revised for Book Two, The Hydra

Christy Zhou: owner and waitress of the New Seattle diner "The Trucker."

* Danielle Arroz: a veteran of the Dirt Star conflicts as a supply warehouse clerk. She becomes a waitress of "The Trucker," a diner in New Seattle on the planet Jook-Sing.

* Liu Zhi: a gifted engineer and test pilot, member of the Jook-Sing military with high-level clearances to top-secret information.

*Abner Oaks: previously a citizen of The Commonwealth. Born to the soil producing ship the Dirt Star. A veteran of the Dirt Star Conflicts. He eventually settled on the planet Jook-Sing, becoming one of the leaders of the Róngyù Shǒuhù Zhě and captain of the starship the Ulysses.

*Louie the Lemon-Filled: a sentient, lemon-filled donut fried into birth aboard the Dirt Star. After a genetic experiment failure, his DNA was accidentally blended with human DNA. Now fully human (with a bit of lemon zest). He also joined the ranks of the Róngyù Shǒuhù Zhě on Jook-Sing and became the owner of a small chain of donut shops.

*Claus the Bavarian: Louie's box-mate having a similar outcome after the failures within the landfill. He eventually joined the Jook-Sing Navy.

*Basir the Persian: a delicious cinnamon donut with an accent no one could explain, as he was born in the same donut shop as his box-mates. He, like the others, settled on Jook-Sing, eventually becoming Róngyù Shǒuhù Zhě.

*The Twins, Angie and Maude: box-mate cousins of Basir by the relation of cinnamon. They were known for their good looks and superior intellect—also, veterans of the Dirt Star Conflict and members of the Róngyù Shǒuhù Zhě.

Arush Turgeen: the supervisor of Abner Oaks in the customs, shipping, and receiving department of the Dirt Star.

Gerwald Bonageres: manager of the customs, shipping, and receiving department of the Dirt Star.

*Bob the Plain Cake: another box-mate of Louie and Róngyù Shǒuhù Zhě.

*Rob the Glazed Old-Fashioned: another box-mate of Louie and Róngyù Shǒuhù Zhě.

Nomar Eleeskee: an E-Tollian brewmaster, freighter captain, and ortric farmer. Friend of Abner Oaks from the system closest to the Commonwealth, the Gomane. Owner of the eflume Cedric.

Undra Eleeskee: beloved late wife of Nomar Eleeskee.

*Jenny Acorn: a Dirt Star facilities technician, Veteran of the Dirt Star Conflicts. She eventually became shifu of the Róngyù Shǒuhù Zhě.

*Flip: a fish-man. another product of the failed experiment of the landfill. A member of Róngyù Shǒuhù Zhě and owner of a fishing charter company.

*Loaf: a meatloaf-man. another product of the failed experiment of the landfill. Sharing DNA with Commonwealth fighter Captain Ramar Gleek, he becomes a Róngyù Shǒuhù Zhě and starship pilot.

Ambassador Xytist Donclees: an ambassador of the planet E-Toll. An official granted the use of the ambassador class ship, the Ulysses, one of the most valuable ships in existence.

Captain Cletus Cudrowe: captain of the Dirt Star.

*Captain Marcus Filet: a Quandrosite and an employee of Ambassador Donclees. The official captain of the Ulysses. He is transformed, humbled and joins the Róngyù Shǒuhù Zhě upon Jook-Sing.

Enfreck Fren: the Dirt Star's facilities department dispatcher.

Wildrew Meeks: a Dirt Star security guard.

Delt: a Dirt Star facilities technician.

Officer Daley: a co-worker security guard of Wildrew Meeks.

Captain Ramar Gleek: a fighter squadron captain of the Dirt Star's Division 2 Security Force of the Commonwealth Defense Force.

Major Hicks: Captain Gleek's commanding officer.

Professor Jamus Lantooto: genetic scientist of the Dirt Star.

Hank Thomas: the Dirt Star's head of security.

Jimmy Roberts: a facilities department engineer of the Dirt Star.

The Yeasts/The Collective: the engineered yeasts present within the landfill used in the production of soil. They were changed by the failed genetic treatments within the landfill. Needing hosts, they possessed the bodies of anyone with whom they came in contact.

Janice: Captain Cudrowe's secretary.

The 41st Red and the 30th Gray: two Commonwealth security battalions present aboard the Dirt Star.

Major Lars Myhra: leader of the Commonwealth 30th Gray Battalion.

Major Vess: leader of the Commonwealth 41st Red Battalion.

The Seals: an abused cousin of the Yeasts. a product derived from a fungus, modified to become fungus-based polymers or FBPs.

Kurts: a highly decorated soldier of the 30th Gray Battalion.

The Bacteria: a lesser-motivated force than that of the Yeasts.

Jennifer Stanley: aka Jenny Acorn.

Professor Timothy Stanley: Ph.D. of Experimental and Observational Astrophysics, Cosmology, and Experimental Particle Physics; father of Jennifer Stanley.

William Stanley: father of Professor Timothy Stanley and grandfather of Jennifer Stanley.

Jennifer Stanley Sr.: mother of Dr. Timothy Stanley; grandmother of Jennifer Stanley.

Angela Stanley: daughter of William and Jennifer Sr.; sister of Timothy.

Adam Daxler: the genius friend of Dr. Timothy Stanley and engineer of 'the Machine.'

Kirsten Stanley: wife of Dr. Timothy Stanley; mother of Jennifer Stanley.

Professor Gerard' t Hooft : (Non-fiction reference was taken from Wikipedia): Gerardus (Gerard) 't Hooft (Dutch: [ˈɣeːrɑrt ət ˈɦoːft]; born July 5, 1946) is a Dutch theoretical physicist and professor at Utrecht University, the Netherlands. He shared the 1999 Nobel Prize in Physics with his thesis advisor Martinus J. G. Veltman "for elucidating the quantum structure of electroweak interactions."
His work concentrates on gauge theory, black holes, quantum gravity, and fundamental aspects of quantum mechanics. His contributions to physics include proof that gauge theories are renormalizable, dimensional regularization, and the holographic principle.

Foster Dex: facilities technician of the Dirt Star. The adoptive father of Jenny Acorn; Husband of Sophia (below).

Physicist Professor Sophia Dex: adoptive mother of Jenny Acorn, wife of Foster Dex.

Dr. Margaret Frost: sneezed on Angie and Maude before their change.

Retired Admiral Torquil Myhra: father of Major Lars Myhra. Took a bite out of Claus before his change.

*Layerie: a rejected lasagna-thing genetic human hybrid who finds his value as a member of the Róngyù Shǒuhù Zhě.

Maurice: a rat-man. after his genetic change, he eventually settled on Jook-Sing, becoming a hairstylist.

*Peanut and Jelly: sibling mouse-people. they, too, are affected by the genetic failure, becoming human/rodent hybrids. They also join the Róngyù Shǒuhù Zhě upon Jook-Sing. Jelly becomes navigator of the starship the Ulysses and shifu of New Seattle's junxio.

Píng Cheng: senior co-shifu with her husband Chen of New Seattle's Junxio for the Róngyù Shǒuhù Zhě.

Chāo Cheng: Ping's other half and fellow seasoned war veteran Róngyù Shǒuhù Zhě.

Florance: greeter within the Dejeal Lock Authority.

Swaying Reed: one of the seven octogenarian Shǒuhù Zhě masters. A willowy Asian woman named Yáoyè De Shù

Iron Ankle: one of the seven octogenarian Shǒuhù Zhě masters. A fierce warrior named Martin Lim.

The Drestak Anai Eb-eb: a princess of the planet Dejeal.

The Castack Lou Eb-eb: the King of the planet Dejeal.

Lux Aequus: King of the planet Crehl.

Lucerna Ignis: Queen of the planet Crehl.

Mactus: Head servant in the Palace of Crehl.

Keith Glemick, Jason Royce, and Gene Fry-The Three: the three most loyal Tolkites to "The Monster" Brian Jung.

About the Author

Erik R. Eide was born in the Chicago area. California's coast became his habitat before Seattle came to be a second hometown. He currently lives in San Antonio, Texas. His passions include faith, family, writing, music production and meatloaf.

Contact

Web:
eideologically.com

Facebook:
Erik R. Eide

Instagram:
erik_r._eide

Twitter
@eideological

Snail
Erik R. Eide
1308 Common St. suite 205, #403
New Branfels, TX 78130

Made in the USA
Monee, IL
27 December 2020